The

Queen Bee

of

Bridgeton

Leslie DuBois

ISBN: 0615460534
ISBN-13: 978-0615460536

Dedicated to all my little Queen Bees
AH class of 2008

Leslie DuBois

Chapter 1
Caught in the Noose

"Every student who has faced this honor council has been found guilty and expelled," Headmaster Collins said from behind the judge's bench of Dardem Hall. Though I knew the expulsion rate of Bridgeton Academy, I prayed the outcome of my own honor trial would be different. I mean, innocence had to account for something, right?

I felt like everyone in the world was staring at me. Probably because they were. The five members of the honor council, which included my sister Sasha, sat in the middle of the stage waiting for my explanation of events. She held her face in her hands shaking with tears as she, too, knew my fate. My accuser smiled smugly, crossed his arms, and winked at me. It was obvious he knew I was innocent. But did that matter?

I cast my eyes down to avoid their gaze, but the view wasn't much better. My pink ballet tights totally clashed with my green plaid school uniform skirt. What was I thinking?

Lucky tights or not, this was a major fashion faux pas. I couldn't bear to look at myself anymore, but looking into the sea of Bridgeton uniforms in the audience was even worse. I caught a glimpse of Ashley's evil little face. I wondered if she noticed the tights too or did her smirk just reveal the utter joy she found in my obvious suffering.

"Sixteen years ago, in my first year here at Bridgeton, I expelled half the senior class along with eleven juniors and three sophomores. I do not tolerate dishonorable actions on my campus." Headmaster Collins continued informing me and the audience of things we already knew. Things he reminded us of constantly every Monday morning in the weekly honor speech.

God, I wanted to be off that stage. I wanted to be anywhere else in the world. Why couldn't I be dancing with the Russian Ballet instead? Hell, I'd take dancing in my tiny bedroom in Venton Heights with gravel in my pointe shoes over this torture. I mean, at Bridgeton, being called a cheater was worse than being called a bank robber or a murderer or a Democrat.

Ashley tapped Lauren on the shoulder, whispered something into her ear, then they giggled hysterically while staring at me. Even through her evilness, Ashley was still beautiful. With her flowing blonde hair and soft blue eyes she looked exactly like Alice from Alice in Wonderland, except with a hint of skank.

Like a queen on her throne, Lauren tossed her curly golden brown hair over her shoulder and shared the joke with Brittany who sat on her other side. Brittany's eyes expanded while she laughed, exaggerating her already horse-like features.

Headmaster Collins banged his gavel. "Is there something you would like to add to these proceedings, Ms. DeHaven?" he said to Lauren in the front row.

"Oh no, sir," she said with syrupy sweetness. "My classmates and I were just commenting on how wonderful it will be when our school is free of people who don't appreciate honesty and virtue." She smirked at me. I wanted to jump off the stage and slap the sneer off her face. But that wouldn't have helped the situation.

I had to admire their ingenuity, somewhat. I mean, to frame me for cheating and have video footage. Pretty genius. If I was more like them, this whole thing probably would never have happened. But I'm not. A poor, black girl from Venton Heights could never defeat the likes of Ashley, Brittany and Lauren. I shouldn't have even tried.

My father used to tell me being black was not a negative no matter how the media portrayed us. He told me I should "Say it loud, 'I'm black and I'm proud.'" I tried to feel that way, but sometimes I just didn't think it was true. I mean, if nothing is wrong with being black, then why did no one want to be 'blacklisted', 'blackballed', or blackmailed? Why is Angel food cake white and Devil's food cake black?

Of course, a black man *did* get elected president. That helped my self-image a little, but not much. I mean, it wasn't a fair comparison. I'm pretty sure Barack and Michelle didn't grow up in Venton Heights. When Homeless Murray from the alley behind my apartment becomes president, then maybe I'll feel comfortable celebrating my blackness.

I needed to concentrate and figure out how to make them believe me. But how could I explain away the video footage those bitches had concocted? Students had been convicted and expelled for much less. I was surprised Headmaster Collins went through this formality at all since he seemed so ready to expel students all the time.

Headmaster Collins, or Colonel Collins as he was sometimes called, scared the pee out of me figuratively and literally.

Once, during my first week at Bridgeton, I inadvertently stepped into a class already in progress just to avoid passing him in the hallway.

Everyone in the class stared at me like the complete moron I was. Even the teacher, with chalk in mid air turned and gave me the classic 'what the hell are you doing?' teacher stare waiting for me to explain my presence. I tried to think quickly as, in my mind, the seconds ticked into minutes, but thinking quickly was not my strong suit. Neither was public speaking. One of two things usually happened when I was caught in a situation like that; either I stood there with my mouth open and eyes bulging as if choking on a chicken bone, or, I started babbling incoherently. That day, I wished for the choking.

"Bathroom...no, I know this is not the bathroom. If it was, then all of you wouldn't be here. Unless it was one of those bathrooms you see in other countries that are just big rooms with several holes and people just squat and go. But all of you people have your clothes on so, I know you're not using the bathroom...um what I mean is that I'm *looking* for the bathroom. Yeah, that's what I mean." I glanced outside the door to see if it was safe to make my exit, but Headmaster Collins had stopped to talk with a faculty member. I had to continue my embarrassing soliloquy long enough for him to pass. "So, bathroom is what I'm looking for because I have to…you know…use it. Not that I can't hold it because I can, I mean I haven't wet myself in like…" just then Headmaster Collins passed and without even finishing my thought, I darted out of the classroom and away from the scathing eyes of my schoolmates. I tried to convince myself that what had just happened didn't happen, but the raucous laughter emanating from the classroom told me otherwise.

"Was that Sasha?" Someone in the classroom asked as they tried to control their giggles.

"Oh, God no!" someone else said. "Have you ever seen Sasha be that…that awkward?"

"I think that was her sister. What's her name again?"

"No idea."

With Archibald Collins as headmaster, Bridgeton was nicknamed the Ivy League High School of North America. Last year 87% of the senior class went on to Ivy League universities. Eighty seven percent! That's like…okay, I don't know how many students that is. Math is another one of my many weaknesses. But, in any case, 87% was a lot of brainiacs going off to brainy schools to do big brainy things.

Dardem Hall was specially erected by Headmaster Collins to review honor violations. This small scale replica of a court house was built on the east lawn and loomed like a noose above all of our heads just waiting for one of us to figuratively hang ourselves by flouting Headmaster Collins' rules. This was only my second year at Bridgeton, but it seemed to me there were a particularly high number of noose victims. I remembered attending trials for other students and feeling absolutely mortified on their behalf for the humiliation they were suffering. The day of my trial, I felt the same mortification, as well as my own personal humiliation.

"In my opinion," the headmaster continued, "cheating is the worst possible offense. Not only does it bring shame upon this school, but it also degrades your personal character. There is no room in Bridgeton for cheaters." He looked at me and said, "Sonya Garrison, unless you can give us an adequate explanation, you will have to finish your junior year elsewhere."

My heart raced. My hands were hot and slippery with sweat. A knot developed in my throat making it impossible for me to utter a sound. What could I possibly say to get out of this? The imminent doom of a life without a high school education pounded my thoughts, and gave me an agonizing headache. What would I do without a high school diploma? Sasha was going to kill me. After we'd worked so hard to make it out of the projects, I had somehow figured out a way to ruin it. Well, in all fairness, I didn't ruin it. It was completely not my fault. Ashley, Brittany, and Lauren set me up and I knew it. Together queen Lauren and her hoochies made up what's called the Bitch Brigade of Bridgeton. The most feared girls in the school. But why did they have it in for me? Why were they so determined to ruin my life? In order to understand, I'd have to start from the beginning. And I guess the beginning started with dance.

Chapter 2:
Dancing Dream

I remember the day I decided to become a ballerina. I wrote a poem for a third grade contest and won free tickets to see the Houston Dance Company perform in Newark. Actually, the poem was more like a prayer asking God to take me out of the nightmare called Venton Heights. My family had only lived there for two weeks, but I had already been beaten up five times for the offense known as "acting white." Because I didn't know the slang or the words to the latest rap song apparently I wasn't black enough.

We had to move to Venton Heights because the bank foreclosed on our little white house with the red shutters in Jersey City. For two years it was my mother, father, Sasha, and I sharing a two bedroom apartment until my mother kicked my father out. There were a number of reasons why my parents' marriage didn't work, but basically, he just wasn't reliable. My mother couldn't rely on him to pay the bills or pay her enough respect to not cheat on her.

At the dance performance, I remembered being completely mesmerized by the movements of the performers. They didn't just dance, they floated like angels. As they twirled around and leaped ten feet in the air, I could practically see myself on stage with them in the pretty costumes. Every arm movement and leg placement inspired me. What would it be like to move like that? I could barely sit as I started to imitate some of the steps. After the third dirty look from the person next to me, I brought my knees to my chin, hugged my legs, and continued to stare at the stage in awe.

When I got home from the performance, I looked in the phone book and found Ms. Alexander's School of Dance. As the only ballet school near Venton Heights, I knew it would be my only opportunity to receive any ballet instruction.

"Please, Mommy, please. If I don't take dance lessons I'll die!" I pleaded with her late one night when she came home from work. It had to be after midnight but I stayed awake sliding around the kitchen in my socks trying to replicate the movements I'd seen from those angelic dancers. I stretched my legs and flailed my arms and spun around on my tip toes. I tried to look graceful. I probably looked ridiculous.

"Baby girl, I just can't afford it. You know times are tight for me and your father right now. Can't you just take a dance class at school?"

"Yeah, if I wanna be in a rap video or something. They don't teach this kind of dancing. This is ballet, Mommy. It's special and it's beautiful and it takes years of practice. Ms. Alexander's school is my only chance, Mommy, please." My mother sat at the kitchen table, slid her shoes off and massaged her feet. She had worked three double shifts in a row just to make this month's rent. Then, first thing in the morning, she had to go to one of her cleaning jobs.

My mother closed her eyes, sighed, and said, "I'll see what I can do." Two days later, she brought home a pair of second hand ballet slippers. It was all she could do.

She gave me those slippers thinking they would appease me long enough to forget this ridiculous dream. She had every reason to feel that way. She thought this new found desire was just like when I was five and I begged her to buy me a dell. No, not the computer. In fact, I didn't even know what a dell was. I'd just been singing "The Farmer in the Dell" and I decided I wanted to be a farmer so, naturally, I needed a dell. Or, when I was seven and I had just watched Star Wars and desperately needed a light saber because I felt the force and I was definitely a jedi. She thought I would grow out of it, but oh, how wrong she was. I borrowed books and videos about ballet from the library. I collected cans until I had enough money to buy a leotard. I even started hanging out in front of Ms. Alexander's studio watching through the window and imitating everything they did. One day, Ms. Alexander herself grabbed me by the shirt collar and dragged me inside.

"Why you stand window stare? No free show!" I was so scared I thought I would wet myself. I had difficulty understanding her thick Asian accent. She would be so much easier to understand if she used a preposition once in a while. I learned later that Ms. Alexander was Japanese. She preferred to go by her husband's last name because Americans could never say her real name properly.

"I'm sorry. I.. I'm sorry...I didn't know I couldn't watch...I'm sorry." I kept repeating myself like a babbling idiot. At eight years old, I was already almost her height, but her demeanor scared me senseless. Not to mention the fact that she carried a walking stick. It wasn't a cane. It was a stick. It was a huge stick nearly as tall as she was and she looked like she might beat me with it.

"What you want?" she demanded still holding my shirt with one hand and her stick with the other. She was skinny as a rail but so strong I couldn't twist myself loose. I didn't know what to say. I looked around the lobby trying to find an excuse as to why I would be standing outside every day staring in the window. Nothing came to me. I got a glimpse into her office and saw papers lying on the floor. The mess wouldn't have bothered me at all, but I could just hear Sasha's voice in my head telling me for the tenth time in any particular day to clean up my side of the room. She could be such a neat freak sometimes. Then it hit me.

"A job. I..I want a job. Do you need someone to clean?"

"No."

"I...I work for really cheap. In fact, you can just pay me with lessons."

"You dance?"

"I want to." Suddenly she dragged me down the hall and into one of the empty classrooms. There were mirrors everywhere, and the wooden floor was so smooth anyone could move like an angel on it. She let me go then walked over to the stereo.

"Move," she barked after she turned on some music.

"What?"

"You too old. I no teach if you no move."

"Move where?"

"Dance!" she yelled. I jumped and then started moving to the music. She played this beautiful enchanting song I didn't know. Later I learned it was the adagio for Beethoven's sonata Pathetique. It instantly became one of my favorites. I closed my eyes and moved to the music. I didn't know what the movements were or what the steps were called; I just did what I saw all the other dancers do. When I opened my eyes, Ms. Alexander was gone. I thought I must have been so bad she couldn't stand to look at me anymore. I waited and waited. When the song ended I turned to leave the studio, head hanging low with shame and embarrassment when suddenly, she appeared.

"Take this," she said, as she handed me a bundle of leotards, tights, and ballet slippers. "Come tomorrow. Clean mirrors, sweep floors, throw away old magazines. Take beginner class. You clean, you dance, that's it, now go."

And that's how it started. Soon I spent more time in Mrs. Alexander's studio than in Venton Heights. And that was fine with me. Dancing was, without a doubt, the best thing to ever happen to me. It even got me into Bridgeton.

Chapter 3:
The Boy with Sad Eyes

Bridgeton was never my dream. It was Sasha's. She was obsessed with using her brain to escape the ghetto. Starting in fifth grade, she applied every four months like clockwork. She got accepted in seventh grade but only with a partial scholarship. She kept applying until she was finally awarded a full scholarship for her sophomore year. The next year, my sophomore year and her junior year, I applied and got in as well on an arts scholarship. And while Bridgeton was a big improvement over Grover Cleveland High School with its metal detectors, drive by shootings, and constantly overflowing toilets, I still never felt safe or comfortable. I always felt like something was bubbling just under the surface of Bridgeton's pristine façade waiting to attack me. So I invoked the power of anonymity as a protection. As far as the Bridgeton populace was concerned, I was invisible. To anyone who was anyone at Bridgeton, I was no one.

Invisibility had its side effects at times, though. For example, one December day, right after the dismissal bell, I was too afraid to ask Lauren DeHaven to move out of the way so I could get into my locker. I just stood there silently hoping she'd move eventually, but she never even noticed me. She just stood there twirling her cream knit scarf with green fringes around while chatting with Greg Smythe.

"So the money is going to the starving children of Honduras," she was saying in reference to her latest philanthropic fundraiser. Among Bridgeton students, Lauren DeHaven was considered the patron saint of altruism. She was constantly raising money or collecting food or organizing benefit walks of one type or another. Most people completely loved her, but to me, she just never seemed genuine. Sasha thought that all the fundraising was just a way for Lauren to draw attention away from her lackluster grades on her college applications and had nothing to do with actually making the world a better place.

"Wait a minute. At the school-wide assembly you said it was for the children of Haiti," George replied.

"Did I? Silly me." She touched his shoulder playfully and tossed her golden brown hair. "I get all those little hell-holes confused. Anyway, do you think you can get your parents to donate a few thousand?"

"Well, that depends, LD. What's in it for me?"

It wasn't like I was afraid of either of them, I just always avoided talking to Bridgeton students. I had no idea how to even hold a conversation with a Bridgeton student. We had nothing in common, had none of the same experiences in life. I was afraid I'd say something that would reveal where I really came from.

Finally, I just left without accessing my locker. It wasn't until I was on the bus on the way to dance rehearsal that I realized I'd left my pointe shoes in my locker. I slammed my head on the seat in front of me. I needed those shoes. We were doing final rehearsals for the Nutcracker and I was playing Clara. Ms. Alexander would kill me if I showed up unprepared.

It was after five by the time I made it back to campus. Thankfully, all the students were gone. Or so I thought.

As I walked along the hall with sugar plume faeries dancing in my mind, the door to the janitor's closet swung open and smacked me in the face. I sailed to the ground with an ungraceful thud. While on the ground clutching my forehead, a pretty redheaded girl and a cute blond boy stepped out. I recognized the boy although I didn't know his name. Two weeks ago I'd seen him crawling out from under the bleachers with his pants in his hand followed by a different girl.

"Sorry about that," he said, extending one hand to help me up and using the other to tuck in his uniform shirt.

I accepted the offer and let him help me to my feet. Then he gently removed my hand from my forehead and took a look at it.

"No damage done," he said. "You're all good."

Before he turned away, I noticed something…compelling.

"You have sad eyes," I said.

"Sad eyes?" the redhead muttered with a laugh. "God you're such a freak. I can't believe you're Sasha's sister." Then she stormed off. I felt like I probably should've told her that her Bridgeton polo was on inside out, but I couldn't take my eyes off the cute, if not, lewd blond boy.

I could only imagine what he was doing with the redhead in the closet, so he should've been quite happy, but his eyes told a different story.

While staring at me, his lips parted as if to say something, but only a troubled sigh escaped. Then he blinked and shook his head as if coming to his senses. "Maybe you should watch where you're going." He gave me the distasteful glare so common among Bridgeton students. It was a look that said 'I'm better than you.'

I gasped. How could he possibly blame me for this run in?

"And maybe you should...should..." he stormed away before I could think of anything clever to say. Let's face it, it would have taken me all day to think of something anyway.

After retrieving my precious pointe shoes, I decided to take the far stairwell. I didn't want to risk running into Closet Boy again. As soon as I entered the stairwell, I heard crying. I wondered if it was the girl from the closet. Maybe she'd regretted her behavior and felt ashamed for having meaningless sex in a closet. Hmph. Served her right. I instantly felt bad for thinking this. I had no right to judge her. I didn't know the circumstances. Maybe she thought this boy really loved her and that's why she did it. No matter what the case, I hated seeing people in pain. I just had to see what I could do to help.

I went up to the next flight and found the source of

the crying. A dark haired girl was crouched in the corner of the stairwell completely naked and sobbing.

"Oh my God what happened?" I dropped all my belongings then whipped off my coat and covered her with it. I knelt beside her and rubbed her back.

"Nothing. Go away. Just leave me alone," she snapped through the tears. That was obviously a lie. Something had to be wrong. Under normal circumstances no one cowers in the corner of a public stairwell naked and crying. I wasn't about to leave the poor girl alone.

I glanced around and searched for her clothes. They were nowhere in sight.

"Where are your clothes?"

"They took them."

"Who's they? Was it a boy? Were you raped?" Instead of answering she shook her head frantically and started crying harder. I felt my eyes well up. Who would do such a thing? It was below zero outside. How was she supposed to get home naked and in the freezing cold? Where was she supposed to find clothing? I guessed that was part of the cruel, sick joke. How could anyone do this to another human being? I tried to blink away the hot tears welling in my eyes. I needed to focus and help this girl. "Come on, let's get you out of here." I helped her to her feet and let her put my coat on. She was quite a bit shorter than me so the coat covered what it needed to, but she would still freeze outside.

"Wait a minute," I said, reaching for my dance bag. Considering I only cleaned it out about once a year, I was bound to have some sort of clothing in there somewhere. I pulled out a pair of sweat pants and a t-shirt from a dance camp I went to in Spain. They smelled kind of rank, but they were better than nothing.

The girl accepted the clothes silently, her well of tears slowly receding. She slipped on the pants, then turned around to take off the coat and put on the shirt.

"Thank you," she said in a hoarse whisper when she'd finished. Under different circumstances, I could tell she was a really pretty girl. With her pale skin and short jet black hair she resembled Snow White.

"No problem. Do you want me to go call the police?"

Her eyes expanded. "No, God no! I don't know what they'll do to me. No one can know about this. Ever." This mysterious 'they' wielded enough power over this girl to literally make her start shaking.

"You can't let them get away with this."

She fell to her knees and started crying again. "Please, you can't tell anyone about this. Please. I beg you."

I bent down beside her and hugged her. "It's okay. It's okay."

"Promise me you won't tell anyone. Promise!" She was hysterical. I didn't want to make such a promise, but I had to do something to calm her down.

"Okay, I won't tell anyone. I promise."

Her tears subsided again. And after about ten minutes

I was able to coax her into leaving the building.

"Do you live far? Can I help you get home?"

"I have my car. They took my purse, but I have an extra key under the license plate."

When we reached the only car in the parking lot, I thought surely she would succumb to another onslaught of tears. Instead, however, she just stared numbly at the vandalism that violated her red SUV. Someone had spray painted male genitalia all over her car, along with the word SLUT on the hood. I could only assume it was the same 'they' that left her naked and shivering in the stairwell. How could she not want to make them pay for all they'd done to her?

In a daze, she found her spare key and entered her car. Seconds later she sped away. I didn't even find out her name.

Chapter 4:

The Right Thing

The sight of that poor girl weighed heavily on my mind. What if this 'they' wasn't finished with her? What if they came back to finish her off? Though I didn't even know the girl's name, I knew in my heart that nothing she could have done warranted such treatment. For two weeks, I searched the halls for her. She was nowhere to be found. It was like she'd dropped off the face of the planet. How could she just disappear without anyone taking notice? Was she another invisible person like me? Could I miss school for two weeks without causing alarm?

I couldn't hold out any longer. I had to tell someone. I had to find this girl and make sure she was alright. So in an effort to do the right thing, I found myself in one of the most dreaded places on campus. Headmaster Collins' office.

"I'm glad you made an appointment to see me, Sonya. I've been meaning to commend you on how much you've brought up your grades."

"Thank you. Sasha has been helping me."

"You know, Sasha might not always be there for you. You should try to do things on your own sometimes. I bet you don't even know what you're capable of accomplishing."

Why wouldn't she be there for me? We'd always be there for each other. I couldn't imagine my life without my sister. Headmaster Collins cracked his knuckles, yanking me out of my thoughts. "So what brings you to my office today?" Considering I hadn't been in his office since the day of my application tour two years ago, that was a very valid question.

"Um. I saw something that I thought needed your attention."

"Does it involve cheating?"

"No sir, but I think it's even more serious." Headmaster Collins leaned back in his chair and tapped a pen on the desk waiting for me to explain. "Um, two, almost three weeks ago there was a girl in the stairwell. She was naked and crying. Someone had stolen her clothes and then vandalized her car." He leaned forward and stared at me intensely, but didn't say anything. "I don't know her name. And I promised her I wouldn't tell anyone. But I haven't seen her since and I was, I mean, I *am* worried and…and…I thought you should know." I took a deep breath and let it out. It felt so good to finally get the secret off my chest.

Without saying a word, Headmaster Collins stood and walked to his bookcase. He pulled a yearbook off the shelf and handed it to me. Yearbook. Why the heck didn't I think of that?

"If you don't mind, would you take a few moments to flip through the pictures to see if you can find her?"

Considering the girl was pretty distraught when I saw her and the fact that a lot of these white girls looked exactly the same to me, I found three girls that it could have been.

Headmaster Collins studied the three names I picked out and settled on one. "Emmaline Graham transferred two weeks ago. I wonder if this coincides with the incident you describe." He closed the yearbook and pulled out the school directory. "I'm going to arrange an appointment with her parents." He reached for his phone and started dialing. "You may go," he said to me. I bolted out of my seat and headed for the door. But before I left he said, "Ms. Garrison, you did the right thing."

***

Though my sister Sasha and I came from the same parents, lived in the same house, and went to the same school we couldn't have been more different.

"Sonya, sweetie, did you start your English paper?" she asked me one night while I stretched on our bedroom floor. I needed to work on my audition choreography for the DiRisio Academy of Dance in Rome. I was hoping to spend my senior year dancing in Europe and then hopefully get picked up by a dance company.

"The paper is under control," I assured her while rolling from a split to a straddle. Sasha pursed her lips and folded her arms as she leaned on the door jamb. She didn't believe me. She knew 'under control' was my code for 'at least I know what class the paper is for'.

"It's due Thursday."

"Yeah, I know. I found your Post It note reminder on my pointe shoes before ballet class today. Very stalkeresque, way to go."

"You need a good grade on this paper," she said, ignoring my sarcasm.

"I know I need a good grade on this paper," I replied mockingly. "I also need a fantastic audition piece. Do you know how world famous DiRisio is? This is my future. I plan on being a professional *dancer*, ya know, not a professional...englisher...or whatever." Sasha rolled her eyes.

"You see, that's your problem. Everything is dance, dance, dance, with you. You have to have an education too. You have to have something to fall back on in case dancing doesn't work out. What if you break your knee or something, huh? Then where will you be? I'm not gonna be around to take care of you forever." Sasha wagged her index finger at me like I'd just pooped on the floor. I'm surprised she didn't roll up a newspaper and smack me on the head with it.

"I don't need you to take care of me," I snapped. I turned my back to her and did a heel stretch.

"Like hell, you don't. Who do you think got you into Bridgeton?"

"I got in on an arts scholarship, thank you very much."

"They wouldn't have even looked at your application if I hadn't already built up the reputation I have as a quality student. And here you come just ruining it." Sasha sat on her bed and pulled out that God awful daily planner of hers or, as I like to call it, 'her left hand'. It was probably more important to her than her left hand. "You know you got an 82% on your last English test? That's practically failing in my book. According to my calculations, you need at least a 95% on this paper to bring your grade into the respectable range."

I put my head in my hands. She gave me such a headache when she went on her grade rampages. I just wished I could think of something to say to get her off my back. But there was nothing. She was right. If it wasn't for her meticulous organization habits, I probably would've flunked out of Bridgeton after only a week.

Sasha reached for my backpack and I winced. She'd flip once she saw how disorganized I'd let it get. She'd probably spend half an hour just organizing everything before we even started on the paper. It's not like I was messy or anything, okay, my papers were a bit cluttered. I didn't even have separate folders for classes. In my world, everything fell into two categories; dance and not dance.

"What is this, a banana?" She shrieked in disgust as she pulled out a black slimy banana peel from the front pocket of my backpack and held it between two fingers.

"Sasha, please, I have this really cool idea for my third audition piece. Just let me spend 30 minutes working it out then I promise I'll work on the stupid paper."

"A, it's not stupid. B, your 30 minutes will morph into three hours and you won't even crack open a book. I know you." She grabbed my backpack and dumped out the contents on to the floor a.k.a my dance space. "This is insane," she murmured staring at the mess of papers, magazines, tights, etc. escaping my backpack.

I inhaled sharply and bit my tongue. I couldn't win this argument. I wanted to be angry with her, but looking into her eyes, all I saw was the heartbroken little girl being rejected from Bridgeton time after time. It was nothing but her love for me and her overwhelming desire to get out of the ghetto motivating her to be so...so aggravating sometimes.

Sasha's hatred for Venton Heights was ten times stronger than mine. She hated everything about it. She hated the suffocating stench of urine permeating the halls of all the apartment buildings. She hated looking at a brick wall when she opened her bedroom window. She said that brick wall symbolized how her life would go nowhere as long as she lived in this place. She hated going to sleep to the sound of gunshots. She hated the alley she had to walk through to get home where she had to step over the not quite dead bodies of homeless people and crack addicts. But I think most of all, Sasha hated the roaches.

She could shut everything else out if she just closed our bedroom door and turned up her music, but those pesky roaches would still come through the fortress she put around herself. They crawled under our bedroom door and out of power outlets and through air vents. No matter how much Sasha cleaned, they kept coming back. She spent hours on her hands and knees scrubbing the kitchen floor, the refrigerator, the bathroom, the stove, everywhere she thought the critters would congregate and it didn't matter. They kept coming back promising to embarrass us one day. Sasha had already had a close call at Bridgeton once. A roach crawled out of her backpack while she was sitting in class. She told me she froze and almost stopped breathing. Someone screamed; the entire class went into hysterics. Fortunately, no one else saw where it came from.

If Sasha ever became President of the United States one day, which was possible because she was just that determined and brilliant, she would probably mark off the city block containing Venton Heights and, with the strongest military weapon in the world, she'd blow it off the face of the Earth.

We stayed up so late working on my English paper that we both groaned when the alarm went off at five the next morning.

"This is all your fault," I mumbled with my pillow over my face after hitting snooze twice. "I'm exhausted."

"I'm sorry, Sweetie." Sasha sat up and stretched her arms. "I just want the best for you. I want you to be all you can be."

"You want me to join the army?" Sasha threw her pillow at me and laughed.

I fished around my night stand for my favorite ballet pink scrunchie with the tutus on it while Sasha sat up and started brushing her long black hair and staring at her planner. "Oh crap! Is today the third?"

"Yeah, why?

"Desi wants to take me out to breakfast today to celebrate our anniversary."

Desmond Long, Sasha's boyfriend was one of the most eligible black boys in New Jersey. He was smart, well-read, had impeccable manners and was very wealthy. Desmond's father was a civil rights attorney who sued Cracker Barrel for discrimination and got a huge settlement. The Long family was loaded. Desmond drove a classic 1968 Mustang convertible in pristine condition. He offered to pick her up for school every day, but Sasha was too embarrassed to show him where we lived.

"Oh, how sweet," I said. Sasha rolled her eyes.

"We've been celebrating our anniversary for two weeks now. Desi goes a little overboard sometimes."

"Well, a year is a long time for a high school relationship. He just wants you to know he loves you."

Sasha sighed. I guess all was not well in paradise.

"Yeah, I know. Look, I have to hurry to meet him at the restaurant or else he'll try to pick me up or something." Sasha ran into the bathroom and got ready in record time.

"So how is it he still doesn't know where we live after dating you for a year? Doesn't he get curious?" I asked her when she came back in the bedroom.

Sasha shrugged. "Desmond does what I tell him. I told him a year ago to never ask to see where I live and he hasn't." She slipped on her stylish black pumps which I thought were way too dressy for school and said, "I'll see you in school. Don't be late! I love you!" as she dashed out the door.

"I love you, too." And I *did* love my annoyingly perfect, hazel-eyed beauty of a sister. I didn't have a tinge of jealousy toward her. Especially not in her choice of men. While Desmond was kind of cute, he really wasn't my type. He was a little too clean cut and well mannered for me. Desmond and Sasha kind of reminded me of a black Barbie and Ken.

My dream guy was David Winthrop, the thespian of Bridgeton. He usually got the lead part in every play or musical put on by Bridgeton Academy. His chiseled movie star good looks even landed him a role in a shampoo commercial. Whenever I had a little extra money, I bought that brand of shampoo and pretended it was him lathering…never mind.

Anyway, he was also the lead singer of the all boys a capella group. His sweet baritone voice made me melt. I loved everything about him. Even the way his dark wavy hair flopped over his forehead nearly covering his gorgeous green eyes screamed slovenly perfection.

I dreamed that one day David and I would get married, move to New York and live enveloped in the most artistic and culturally rich society the world had to offer. He could star in a show on Broadway while I danced as principal for any of the billion famous dance companies in New York. Eventually, I would take a couple of years off and pop out a few kids just as David was discovered by Jerry Bruckheimer who was in the audience for one of his shows. Mr. Bruckheimer would be so impressed by his performance he would ask David to star in his next movie. So then, David and I and the kids would be whisked off to Los Angeles and thrown into the Hollywood scene. After David won his first Oscar, I would be ready to start dancing again so we would need to move back to New York. But by this time, David would be so famous that he's asked to star in a TV show based there so we could both work again.

We would have such a glamorous and romantic life. I had it so well planned out I almost forgot the one minor hitch. David literally had no idea I existed. The only time he had ever spoken to me, he thought I was Sasha. Actually, a lot of people thought I was Sasha. I guess we looked more alike than I thought. I took it as a compliment since she was absolutely gorgeous. Anyway, I was too awestruck by David to correct his mistake. I just smiled and nodded and relayed the message to Sasha while we ate lunch.

"By the way, David Winthrop wants to meet you at 4:15 in the Physics lab."

"When did you talk to David?" Sasha asked, looking up from her planner for the first time since we sat down under our favorite tree on the West Lawn.

"Well, I didn't really talk to him. He talked and I smiled and nodded like an idiot. The whole time he thought I was you."

"Look," Sasha said as she closed her book, "I know you have this thing for him, but he's really not for you. He's a rather unsavory character and you should stay away from him."

"What do you mean?"

"Just trust me, Sweetie. I'm looking out for you. I know what's best." Sasha looked at her watch and said, "I gotta go, I have an honor council meeting."

It didn't surprise me that Sasha was trying to tell me who I should or shouldn't date. She always took care of me.

But Sasha forbidding me to pursue David made me want him even more. It did make me wonder, however, if David was such an unsavory character, as she put it, why was she meeting him at 4:15 in the Physics lab?

Chapter 5:
The Return of Closet Boy

"Late again, Ms. Garrison?" Headmaster Collins said as I tried to sneak in the side door of the McIntyre Building. Okay, really he didn't *say* it as much as he *barked* it making me nearly jump right out of my skin.

"Um…I…," I really didn't know how to respond to this. I mean, if I said 'no', well, that would just be a lie. The bell rang like ten minutes ago. And if I said 'yes', well I was pretty sure Headmaster Collins had learned many ways to kill a person and I didn't want him to try one of them on me.

"That's the fourth time this week," he added as he crossed his arms over his huge chest. I think he grew three inches just in the last five seconds.

"Um…I…,"

"Would you like to explain yourself?"

"Um…yeah…I," I looked down at my untied laces. I hoped he didn't notice the sneakers. They were against the dress code. Ladies had to wear dress shoes with their uniform. But it wasn't very comfortable to wear dress shoes when your mornings were as hectic as mine. Every morning, I woke at five, threw on some sweats and caught a bus to Ms. Alexander's studio. It was a half hour ride, but at least it was on the way to school. I spent about an hour cleaning the place from top to bottom. I swept the floors, organized Ms. Alexander's office, took out the trash and cleaned all the mirrors. And there were a ton of mirrors.

Anyway, when I finished cleaning each morning, I took advantage of having the place to myself and I did what I loved. I danced. I turned up the Chopin or the Tchaikovsky so loud I couldn't even hear myself think. Then I closed my eyes and imagined I was Natalia Karleskaya of the Russian Ballet. When I was eight, I saw a video of the Russian Ballet performing Romeo and Juliet. The video was like twenty years old and the quality was crappy, but one thing was quite clear: Natalia Karleskaya was the best ballerina I had ever seen or would ever see. I fell in love with her dancing. To see her dance was like having an exquisite ocean wave of loveliness pound against the walls of my heart. Simply breathtaking. It made me want to weep. I knew I'd never be able to dance like her. Ms. Alexander believed I had the potential and that I should never give up trying. She thought that one day I'd be able to dance right alongside of Natalia Karleskaya or maybe even replace her. I didn't agree. But it was fun to dream.

Headmaster Collins quickly tired of my incoherent

stuttering and told me he was revoking all of my upperclassmen privileges. That just basically meant I couldn't leave campus during my free periods. Since I never left campus anyway it wasn't really much of a punishment. I had no friends and nowhere to go. Besides, I preferred to explore the grounds of Bridgeton Academy than go out to a sandwich shop or coffee house for a few minutes. There was always something interesting to see on the 1500 acre campus. Sometimes I walked to the stables and watched students take riding lessons. Or I'd go to the fountain outside the observatory and make a wish while tossing in a coin. My wishes always consisted of one or two things. Either to dance with the Russian Ballet next to Natalya Karleskaya or to have David Winthrop notice me. Either of which would have been a miracle.

Yeah, there was always something to do on Bridgeton's beautiful campus. Staying on it during my free periods was no punishment at all. If possible, I would live there to avoid having to go home to Venton Heights.

"Um, Sir?" I said before he walked away. "Did you find out who hurt Emmaline?"

He shook his head. "I've spoken to her every week for over a month. She refuses to talk."

"So that's it? They're just going to get away with it?"

"The people who did this have no honor. Their actions will reveal their true character soon enough."

***

That afternoon, while waiting for Sasha to meet me, I

sipped a latte. I was completely exhausted and thoroughly surprised and proud that I had made it through the entire day without falling asleep in class after staying up so late with her. I was daydreaming about my audition for The DiRisio Academy of Dance in Rome when the oddest thing happened. A boy, a cute boy approached me and just stood at my table. From the green blazer and khakis I knew he was a schoolmate, but it took me a second to actually recognize who he was. He was the boy from the closet two months ago. I checked out his eyes. They were still sad.

"My psychiatrist says I should go out with you," he said out of the blue. There was no 'hi, how are you today' or even 'hi, my name is.' I looked over my shoulder then pointed to myself. He couldn't possibly be talking to me. But he nodded and said, "Yes, you."

"Well, that is the worst pick up line I have ever heard in my life." I took another sip of my latte and tried to ignore his presence.

"That's because it's not a pick up line. It's the truth. Well, actually, he didn't specifically say to go out with you, but he did say to get to know you. He thinks it'll be good for me."

I stared at him in disbelief for a moment. He had taken off his jacket and slung it over his shoulder like a model in some sort of commercial for toothpaste or apple pie. He looked just that perfect with his crisp white shirt and khakis that looked a little too big, but gave him an aura of relaxed confidence. He seemed cool, self-assured and…rich except for his shoes. They were beat up red Converse All-Stars. They really didn't match the image he portrayed.

Was he serious? This had to be some sort of joke. But he didn't crack a smile. I think he was serious, which meant I had to set him straight.

"Um, no," I said with finality. But I could tell this guy was not used to taking no for an answer.

"And why not?" He didn't sound surprised or angry. In fact, he sounded kinda full of himself. As if any second he was going to elicit the response he wanted.

"Because I don't know anything about you. Oh, wait, let me correct that. I do know you frequent closets and other sketchy places and do…things with random girls."

"Is that really all you know about me?"

I nodded. "Yes, that's all I know. Is there more?"

He paused for a moment as if he was really thinking about this question. He opened his mouth to speak, but just like the time at the closet nothing came out but a tortured sigh. Something was really bothering this boy. Part of me wanted to find out what it was and help him, but another part of me wanted to get as far away from this high school playboy as possible.

"Listen, Closet Boy, I don't know why you and your shrink are talking about me, but -"

"Closet Boy? You don't know my name?"

I shook my head.

"You really have no idea who I am, do you?"

"Should I?"

"God, you're adorable."

"What?" I slammed my latte down on the table splashing some of it on my dance magazine. "Look whatever your shrink is doing, tell him it's not working. You got some serious problems."

"Yeah, I know," he said, turning and walking away. "I'll pick you up at seven," he called out over his shoulder.

"No, no you won't!" I yelled after him. "I'm not going out with you. I have to dance tonight." He didn't even acknowledge me.

I was so busy staring at him and wondering what kind of crazy he was that I didn't notice when Sasha arrived.

"Why were you talking to Will Maddox?"

I shrugged. "Is that his name? I had no idea. He just came over here and asked me out."

"What do you mean he asked you out?" Sasha pulled out a chair, plopped down into it, then leaned toward me ready to hang on my every word.

"What part of that sentence is hard to understand, Sasha? I mean he asked me out."

"On a date?"

I rolled my eyes. "Yes, on a date. Why is that so hard for you to believe?" That was actually a dumb question cause it was kind of hard for even me to believe. No one had ever asked me out on a date before. Ever!

"Well, because it's Will Maddox. He never asks girls out. He doesn't have to. Girls throw themselves at him." Sasha leaned back in her chair for a moment and chewed on her thumb knuckle. I went back to flipping through my now damp dance magazine and putting this Will person out of my mind. He was definitely not for me. I had seen with my own eyes how he treated girls. I didn't want to be his next closet conquest. As far as I was concerned, this supposed date with Will was a non issue. It just wasn't going to happen. That was until I saw a spark in Sasha's eye. She was cooking up something. "Do you know what one date with Will can do for your social status?"

"No, I don't know. Who is this guy anyway?"

"He's WILL MADDOX," she said through clenched teeth like I was supposed to know exactly what that meant.

"Sorry, that means nothing to me."

Sasha rolled her eyes. "He's only been at Bridgeton for two years and he's already a legend. He's the star of the basketball team and probably the hottest boy on campus."

"I guess he's kinda hot, but David is hotter." I turned the page of my dance magazine and saw what seemed to be a fascinating article on ballet slippers with arch support.

Sasha stared at me with her mouth agape. "I can't believe you're treating this so nonchalant. This is huge, Sonya, huge! We have to figure out what you're gonna wear."

"No we don't."

"And you're gonna need these," she said, digging into her purse. She handed me some little foil packages.

"Condoms? I don't need these." I crammed them back into her purse.

"You most certainly do need them. They don't call him Will the Drill for nothing."

Now I was even more convinced that I would not be going out with this boy. "Sasha, I don't need them because I told him no."

"You did what?" she screamed, leaping from her seat. When everyone turned their head to stare at her she regained her composure and sat down demurely. "Nobody says no to Will Maddox."

"Well, just call me Nobody." That didn't come out quite right.

***

Pointe class ran a little over that night. It was supposed to end at seven, but Ms. Alexander kept pushing us full tilt well past 7:15. Not that it mattered really. I had nowhere else to be. It did cut into my time to eat dinner before my next class, but considering I only had seventy-eight cents to my name, I really couldn't afford to go buy a meal anyway. All I needed was fifteen minutes or so to hit up the vending machine down the street. That would have to last me until I got home. My stomach grumbled in protest of the vending machine entrée but I didn't have a choice. I didn't want to bother Ms. Alexander for a few dollars, especially considering she already overpaid me for the cleaning and the side classes I taught. I already owed her too much.

I walked out onto the sidewalk and noticed a very attractive blond boy leaning on a black BMW and holding a huge bunch of white roses. At first it didn't even cross my mind that the blond boy was waiting for me, but when he walked toward me, I instantly recognized Closet Boy.

"Here," he said, stuffing three dozen roses in my face.

"What the...why the...how the..." I stuttered.

"It's 7:27. We had a date at 7."

"No, we did *not* have a date. I'm dancing," I said, gesturing to the studio behind me.

"Your pointe class ended at 7. You're free until 8 when you teach the adult beginner class."

"You're a stalker. You're a psycho stalker, aren't you?" I took a step away from him back toward the studio.

"Possibly. Or...maybe I just read the schedule on the door. Either way, it doesn't change the fact that I want to get to know you better."

I turned and took a look at the schedule. Okay, so it did have the class times and my name as the instructor of the eight o'clock class. The question still remained how he knew where I danced in the first place.

"Why? Why me?"

"Let me buy you dinner...a quick dinner...and I'll tell you."

I clutched my stomach as it made an audible growl.

"I'm hungry and broke, so I'll go with you to an eating establishment and I'll sit with you and I'll let you pay. But it's not a date."

Chapter 6:
The Weird Date

We went to Kotchy's Deli three doors down from the studio. I sat at a booth and placed my huge bouquet of flowers next to me, while Will went and grabbed us a bite to eat. When he returned to the table, I dug into the meatball sub he'd bought me without waiting for him to even unwrap his turkey club. That's another reason why I was confident this wasn't a date. If it was a real date with a guy I really kinda liked I would've been too nervous to let him actually see me eat. If I ever started dating David I was sure to lose a ton of weight.

"I don't like myself very much," he began suddenly. I would've asked why, but my mouth was full of food. Thankfully, he kept talking. "That day I knocked you over with the closet door...the way you looked at me...it was like you could see through me. Like you could see the real me. That's something *I* can't even see anymore."

I swallowed and said, "The door just probably

knocked something loose in my head. It was nothing."

"And then you said I had sad eyes," he said, ignoring my response. "And…and you're exactly right." He sighed and stared at his still tightly wrapped food. "So I wanted to know how is it that someone I'd never spoken to or even seen before could know me with just one look. So, yes, I kinda started stalking you."

My eyes expanded and I nearly choked on a new bite of food.

"Don't worry, I haven't been watching you undress or anything. I mean the only place you go is to that dance studio. So, I've watched you dance. Sometimes on Sundays you're in the studio for hours and I'll stand across the street and watch you through the window. The way you close your eyes and let the music move you, you seem so free, so at peace. And it makes me feel the kind of peace I haven't been able to feel in years."

Will took out his sandwich and carefully cut it into three pieces. Then he separated his fries into three piles.

"Here, eat this," he said, handing me a French fry.

"Why?"

"There are sixteen."

"So?"

"Sixteen isn't divisible by three."

I didn't know why that mattered but I took the fry anyway and ate it.

"What I'm trying to say is that," he took a deep breath and let it out slowly. "I think you're unique, talented, beautiful, kind, and even a little weird sometimes."

"Weird?"

"Yes, weird. I like weird."

"I'll tell you what's weird. This date is weird."

"Oh, so you admit this is a date?" He smiled. Wow, he had a gorgeous smile. No wonder he easily got what he wanted from women. I barely knew him, but one glimpse of his smile made my stomach pirouette.

"I have to go now," I said, glancing at my watch.

"You still have ten minutes. Just sit and eat with me and then I'll walk you back."

Already nearly done with my food I sat back and watched him devour his. He seemed to eat with some sort of calculated method. He started with the center pile of food, ate the sandwich then the middle French fry then one to the right, then one to the left, then right, then left. Then he repeated the process with the right pile of food. Before he started on the last pile I said, "Why are you telling me all this? You don't even know me, but you're telling me that you have a psychiatrist, you're sad, and you're part stalker. What if I tell other people? Wouldn't that ruin your basketball superhero status?"

He swallowed and said, "First of all, I've played basketball my entire life. It's the only thing that keeps me from going completely insane. I never asked for 'superhero status' as you call it. I'll play no matter what people think of me. Second of all, I know you won't tell people. You're not like that."

He was right about that much. This boy obviously had problems and I wasn't the type of person to go proclaiming them to anyone who would listen. I felt his pain. I couldn't imagine what kind of agonizing secrets lay hidden under his popular boy façade.

We walked back to the studio in silence. It was such an awkward date, that is, if I wanted to call it a date. It only lasted a few minutes, but I felt so connected to him already. And I had to admit I felt pretty special still holding my roses. I had never gotten flowers from a boy before. He was so different from what I imagined him to be. Deep down I knew I really wanted to know him about as much he wanted to know me.

"Can I give you a ride home when you finish here tonight?" he asked once we stood in front of the studio.

Crap. He wanted to take me home. I couldn't let him do that. Sasha would kill me. Hopefully, he hadn't stalked me enough to already know where I live. Plus, I had just met this guy. For all I knew he could be a serial killer. A cute serial killer, but a serial killer nonetheless. I didn't want him knowing where I lived so soon.

"No, that's alright. I'll be fine."

"Can I call you tonight?"

"I don't have a cell phone and my home phone is…" I didn't want him to know my phone was disconnected because we couldn't pay the bill. Not having enough money for a snack is one thing; not being able to pay your phone bill is just plain embarrassing. "My home phone is broken," I said simply, hoping he wouldn't press the issue further.

"Can I give you a ride to school in the morning?"

I sighed. I felt bad saying no to all of his polite requests. He suddenly looked like a wounded little boy. I decided on a compromise. "How about you meet me here in the morning and we can ride to school together?"

"That'll work," he said with a brightness entering his eyes. "I'll see you at a quarter to seven." He turned toward his car, but then stopped, turned and gave me a quick peck on the cheek. "Good bye, Sonya."

Chapter 7:

Like the Car

I stayed at the studio so late that night that I missed the last bus. Which meant I had to walk home to Venton Heights. Alone. I hated that. I literally feared for my life. That was not the way it should be. No one should be terrified of where they lived. Sasha wasn't afraid. She fit in so well, she knew no one would mess with her.

"Hey, white girl," I heard LaPorscha Bennett call as I walked through Venton Heights after midnight. That was her nickname for me. Ever since my first day in Venton Heights she thought I acted like a stuck up white girl and she took it upon herself to give me daily reminders of who I was and where I came from. Things got worse when I became skilled in ballet. She would take my dance bag and ruin my leotards and shoes.

LaPorscha's daily reminders became more physical in

the fifth grade after Boo Man gave me a Valentine's Day card. Tyrell Fitts earned the nickname Boo Man because of his uncanny ability to just appear when people least expected it and scare them half to death.

Unbeknownst to me, Tyrell was LaPorscha's man. I was naively unaware that a fifth grader could stake claims on men or that a fifth grade boy could even be considered a man. In any case, I had committed an unforgivable grievance against LaPorscha. Six years later she was still seeking revenge over a fifth grade romance. LaPorscha had a two-year-old son from Tyrell, but for some reason she still saw me as a threat.

"White girl, I'm talking to you." I could hear the animosity in her voice. I quickened my pace and focused on my apartment building. Just a few more paces and I would be there.

I actually found myself wishing Tyrell would mysteriously appear as he often times did. Underneath his hard gang banger exterior loomed a really nice guy. Over the years, he'd developed into one of the most powerful gang members in the neighborhood, but not by physically fighting his enemies. He used other methods of intimidation to keep control of his area and somehow he always knew what went on with everyone everywhere. When he was around, all he had to do was look at a person to put them in their place. When he was around, LaPorscha paid no attention to me. Unfortunately, he wasn't around tonight.

"I said, I'm talking to you. Don't ignore me." I could see her out of the corner of my eye. Even if I started running, she could catch me. I felt the inevitability of a fight creep up my spine and tense my neck. It had been about six or seven months since my last run in with her, I guess I was due for another brawl. It came with the territory, one of the requirements of living in Venton Heights. I stopped walking, sighed and turned to her.

"You think you're too good to talk to me now that you go to that rich white school?" There was no right answer to a question like that. If I said yes, well, that was a beat down. And if I said no, well, she wouldn't believe me anyway, and that was still a beat down.

"Why don't you go take care of your son, Saturn, or Mitsubishi or whatever the hell his name is?" I tried to sound brave even though tears welled behind my eyes just waiting to gush forth. Her son's name was Tercel, like the car. I thought it was ridiculous for people to name their children after automobiles, but I guess she wanted to carry on the tradition.

LaPorscha swung at me and I dodged it. I had gotten into so many fights with that girl that I basically knew all of her moves. I could honestly say I even had a few victories under my belt.

As always, LaPorscha grabbed my hair and threw me to the ground. She climbed on top of me and started punching me in the face. I reached through her arms, grabbed a fistful of hair and pulled so hard I thought I might have ripped out her weave. She screamed in agony as I kicked her off of me with both legs. I scrambled to my feet and ran home.

"What happened?" Sasha asked as I burst into our

bedroom. I was shaking so hard I couldn't even respond. "Was it LaPorscha?" she asked as she sat me down on the bed and hugged me. I nodded. "It's okay, sweetie. Sasha's here."

"Oh no...my bag!" I suddenly realized I'd entered the apartment empty handed. "I have a brand new pair of pointe shoes in there. They cost me seventy-five dollars. I can't afford a new pair. I need my shoes."

"Don't worry, I'll get them." Sasha stood up and started changing out of her nightclothes.

"But she could still be out there," I said fearing what LaPorscha would do to her. Sasha gave me a 'so what if she is' kind of look and continued changing.

"It's about time that bitch learned to leave my sister alone," she said as she quickly wound her hair into a bun and dashed out the door.

Two hours later Sasha plopped my dance bag on my bed and said, "LaPorscha will never bother you again."

And she didn't.

Chapter 8:
Fat Tuesday

Will showed up at the studio the next morning right after I'd finished vacuuming the lobby. He carried a bagel, a vanilla latte, and more flowers. This time white calla lilies. "Good lord, Will. More flowers? Did you rob a florist?" I asked when I let him in the studio.

He smiled. "Nope. No need for violence. They respond kindly to cash."

I let him have a seat while I went to find a vase. "You don't have to bring me flowers every time you see me," I said when I returned.

"For the past two months, I've been nothing but 'Closet Boy' to you. I figure I have a lot of work to do to change your opinion of me. If that means buying you flowers and food every day, so be it." He held up the bagel and the latte.

"Great, in a few days I'm gonna be a fat flower expert." I sat down next to him on the lobby bench and bit into the bagel.

"So why do you have to clean this place anyway?" he asked, looking at the vacuum with distaste.

"I don't *have* to clean it. I do it in exchange for lessons. It's an arrangement Ms. Alexander and I worked out when I was eight."

"Why do you even need lessons? You're the most amazing dancer I've ever seen. Why don't you just put on your own shows and get rich?"

I laughed out loud. And I thought I was naïve about things. "Thanks for the compliment, but I'm not *that* good. Not yet, anyway. And it's extremely difficult to make a living as a professional dancer. My favorite ballerina, Natalia Karleskaya of the Russian Ballet has been in the business for over twenty years. She's been a principal dancer for most of her adult life and she's still by no means rich. A true dancer doesn't do it for the money. They do it because they can't *not* do it. For me, dancing is like an elegant stream of life-giving water. It nourishes my soul. Without it, I'd shrivel up and die."

Will didn't respond. He just stared at me with his blue eyes filled with wonder…or confusion. I couldn't really tell.

"I sound like an idiot, don't I? That's why I avoid talking to people as much as possible. I come off, like you said, weird."

"I also said I like weird." His voice was deep and sensual causing my skin to tickle. He leaned toward me, embracing my eyes with a penetrating stare. Suddenly he turned away and cleared his throat. "Believe it or not, I feel the same way about basketball."

"Really?"

"Don't act so surprised. Basketball is a skill just like dance. And when I'm on the court and I hear the ball pounding the pavement, it pounds out all other thoughts and distractions, you know?"

I nodded. I *did* know. I understood exactly what he was saying.

"Follow me," I said, putting down the bagel and grabbing his hand. I led him to one of the classrooms. I left him in the center of the room while I turned on a Brahms Sonata played by Itzhak Perlman.

As the luscious violin tones filled the studio, I tried to show him some moves.

I did a simple right arabesque into devant attitude, then a coupé, a tombé, pas de bourrée into an inside pique turn. "Okay, now you try."

Will just laughed. "Not a chance. I can't move like that."

"Sure you can." I went over to him and straightened his posture. "Now keeping your hips square, just extend your right leg back."

Will tried to obey, but he was a really big guy and not very flexible. He looked kind of like an awkward, gangly giraffe. I had to hold in a giggle as I reached for his leg to adjust his turnout. Unfortunately, I didn't account for his lack of balance in such an unfamiliar position. He started tilting over and though I tried to keep him upright, he was too big for me and I ended up tumbling to the floor on top of him. We both erupted into laughter.

"I think I'll stick to basketball," he said.

"I think that's best for the both of us."

Our laughter subsided as his arm slid around my waist and pulled me closer. His breath caressed my forehead and his heart rate increased underneath me. I felt warm and safe in his arms. I could've stayed there forever, but after a few moments Will said, "We better get to school."

***

I cried a lot. I couldn't help it. I cried when I was happy, sad, scared, or even when I had a certain burst of courage. I cried when I was too angry for words, I cried when I was embarrassed. Songs, books, movies and TV episodes made me cry. It didn't even have to be a sad TV show. I once cried on a rerun of The Simpsons. The one where Bart failed the fourth grade. I just felt so bad for him. And he's a cartoon character!

Sasha said I was too sensitive. She said sometimes you had to get over your emotions and make cold rational decisions in order to get ahead in life. That was certainly true in her case. I just couldn't understand how she could sit on the honor council and hold someone's future in her hands. Just the thought of making the decision to expel someone from school and banish them to a bleak, barren future made my heart ache.

The Monday after Will and I rode to school together, Sasha gave the final vote to expel yet another person from Bridgeton. Someone named Nicole Thomas had sewn a cheat sheet into her skirt. She claimed it was just her study aid and she hadn't used it during the test. A pretty flimsy lie, but I still felt bad for her. She actually started crying on stage, which in turn made me cry. Thankfully, I didn't start weeping while sitting in the audience. It was one of my quiet cries. Only two or three stray tears escaped. I was able to cover them up before anyone saw. Or, so I thought.

"Did you know Nikki?" Will asked me as we filed out of Dardem Hall. I shook my head. "Then why are you crying?" He handed me a tissue.

"Am I crying?" I snatched it out of his hand to clean my face before anyone else saw. "I didn't realize." I felt the need to explain, but I had a hard time finding the right words to express that I was a blubbering idiot who cried at everything. So, I said, "I'm a blubbering idiot," in a resigned matter of fact tone. I couldn't come up with any clever or sophisticated explanation, so I just told the bare honest truth. "I know it's stupid. I'm stupid. I just…I'm just…sensitive I guess."

Will smiled and said, "You're not stupid…" He leaned forward, put his lips to my ear and whispered, "You're special." Then he walked away.

***

The next day before school, I wandered the halls aimlessly thinking of Will. Well, that's not completely true. I did have an aim. I kinda hoped to run into him. In four days, Will had already called me unique, beautiful, talented, kind, weird, not stupid, and special. All David ever called me was Sasha.

Unfortunately, instead of running into Will, I ran into a cow. Yes, a cow. No, I wasn't on a field trip visiting farmers or dells. I was on the third floor of the McIntyre building on the Bridgeton campus and I walked into a cow. A cow! Actually, right before impact, I slipped on something wet, which I will pretend was not cow urine, then I lunged forward and planted my face squarely into the side of the massive foul smelling beast.

I sat on the floor for a second with my hand resting in the wet substance, which, once again, I will assume was not urine even though it felt warm, trying to figure out whether I really just crashed into a cow or whether I had slipped into a really elaborate dream. Before I could decide, Colbert Thornton approached me and frantically inquired, "Where's Sasha?" I really didn't know how to respond to that. For one thing, I didn't know. For another thing, I just had a very physical confrontation with a cow and the cow had won. I was trying to recover while wiping off the liquid that was beginning to smell more and more like urine. How could she be so concerned with my sister's whereabouts when there was a cow standing in the middle of the hallway? A cow!

"You mean that's not Sasha?" the scrawny brunette standing next to Colbert said. I didn't know who she was. I barely knew any of the students at Bridgeton. I only knew Colbert because she was Sasha's vice-president on student council. Last year, when they were running for office, they were constantly together planning their campaign. They had professional banners and buttons made, they handed out flyers describing their platform, they even used Colbert's house as a campaign office and made phone calls to other students in order to insure their vote. Talk about overkill.

All of their efforts weren't needed, however, because Blake Armstrong withdrew two weeks before the election and Leila Baker transferred to another school three days before. Sasha and Colbert won by default.

"Susannah, would Sasha walk into a cow?" Colbert asked as if my awkwardness should have been proof enough I could not possibly be Sasha.

Well, at least I knew I wasn't the only one that saw the cow.

"Sorry, black people look the same to me," Susannah said with a shrug.

I chose to ignore that comment and focus on the "elephant in the room." Well, I guess, literally, it was a cow in the room. I was too confused to ask a logical question. So, in the eloquent and articulate manner only I could accomplish I grunted, "Cow," while pointing at it like a three-year-old.

"Yeah, I can see that." Colbert rolled her eyes and tucked her blond bob behind her ears. She had just gotten it cut and now looked like that little French cartoon character. What was her name? Amanda, Emily, Elise, Eloise?

Suddenly, I wasn't thinking of the cow anymore as I tried to figure out the name of the little French cartoon girl. Madeline? No, that was the other one. Eloise, definitely Eloise. Or maybe I confused the two. Let's see, one was from France and one was from New York.

"Do you know where your sister is or not? It's important," Colbert nearly yelled. Her voice brought me out of my thoughts of cartoon characters and back to the reality that I practically sat under a cow in a urine-like substance I refused to believe was urine.

I looked at the cow then at Colbert then back at the cow and for the life of me, I couldn't figure out why they didn't care a cow was in the middle of the hallway. And why was the cow named Heather according to the sign around its neck?

Colbert and company soon tired of my dumbfounded staring and stormed off leaving me alone with Heather the cow.

"It's the Fat Tuesday Cow," Sasha explained when I caught her outside of her first period class.

"What?" I assumed she meant Fat Tuesday as in Mardi Gras, but I still didn't understand what that had to do with a cow.

"Every year, on Fat Tuesday, someone steals a cow from Mr. Dunn's farm, walks it up to the top floor of one of the buildings and names it after a freshman. You missed it last year. You were on an audition."

"Why would anyone do that?"

"It's a tradition. It takes forever to get the cow out of the building since it won't fit in the elevator and apparently cows are afraid to go down stairs."

"But why do they name it after a freshman?" I asked as the warning bell sounded. Sasha looked at the clock. I knew she worried about me being late to class. Again.

"Well, it's always a freshman who needs a little more…exercise than most."

"You mean they're calling some poor girl a fat cow? That's awful. They could scar her for life." I felt a hard lump develop in the back of my throat. Tears threatened to follow soon. As a dancer, I knew how some girls struggled with body image. Just last year, Grace Younger, a girl from my studio, was hospitalized for anorexia and had to miss the spring recital. "Sasha, this is terrible. Who would do something like this?"

"The Bitch Brigade," she said in her 'duh' voice as if I was an idiot for not knowing.

"Bitch Brigade? You mean they're real?" I'd heard stories about them, but I always thought they were fabrications or exaggerations. To me, the Bitch Brigade was Bridgeton's equivalent of the boogieman.

Sasha rolled her eyes. "Yes, they're real. They're a stupid group of girls who think they own the school. I'll tell you about them later. Right now, you need to get to class."

"I can't go to class. What if Heather sees that cow? Sasha, we have to do something."

"I can't, sweetie. Class is about to start." Sasha may have needed her perfect attendance record, but I really didn't care about mine. What was one more tardy amongst the twenty-seven I had already accumulated this year? She must have read my mind as she looked at the clock and said, "If you're gonna to be late anyway, put on the extra uniform I have in my locker. You smell like urine."

I wished I knew who this Bitch Brigade was so I could replace Heather's name with theirs. But since I didn't know, I had to be satisfied with just taking off Heather's sign and hoping she hadn't seen it or heard about it yet.

Unfortunately, it wasn't as simple as just whipping off the sign. The pranksters probably anticipated someone trying that and the sign was securely attached around the cow's neck with a wire nearly choking it. It bordered on animal cruelty.

No matter how I pulled and tugged, it didn't come off. I needed a wire cutter. But where in the world would I find a wire cutter in the middle of first period on the third floor of the McIntyre building?

I took my blazer off and tied it around the cow's neck covering the name. Then I decided to somehow get the cow out of the building. I remembered Sasha saying that cows were afraid to go down stairs, so I thought if I led the cow down backwards, it wouldn't know it was going down stairs. Amazingly, it worked. It was slow going and awkward, but I definitely got the cow to cooperate. I had to move the back legs down one step then run around to the front of the cow and put the front legs down and repeat one step at a time.

The bell rang signaling the end of first period.

Everyone stared at me and the cow laughing as they passed me on the stairwell. Humiliating, yes, but I didn't care. I just didn't want Heather to feel like a cow for the rest of her life.

I continued to coax the cow down the stairs with tears in my eyes when I heard someone say, "Can I help?" Will had his blazer off and his sleeves rolled up ready to jump in and work. I nodded.

"So, you're pretty good at this," I said after we'd been working in silence for a few minutes. "Have any aspirations to be a professional cow mover?"

Will smiled. "It's definitely a close second on my list of dream jobs."

"What's number one?"

"Well, I'd love to get drafted to the NBA. But given that I'm only six foot and white, I don't think that's gonna happen any time soon. So, I think I might try to sign with a European team and develop my game oversees for a while."

"Europe? I love Europe. I went to a dance camp in Spain one summer. I'm hoping to go there next year too."

"Really? Maybe we'll see each other there."

"Maybe."

Forty minutes into second period, we had the cow out of the building.

"Thanks," I said to him while we stood in the parking lot exhausted.

"No problem. I hate the Fat Tuesday prank. It's cruel. It was sweet of you to try to help." Will's eyes sparkled causing me to blush and fluster.

"You should be in class," Headmaster Collins barked, stepping up behind us.

"I know...I'm sorry...I just...I couldn't...it's a cow," I stuttered.

"It's the Fat Tuesday prank, sir," Will explained. "We were just trying to keep this year's victim from getting hurt." Headmaster Collins stared at us for a moment with a sour expression. I thought we were in such trouble.

"You should still be in class."

I dropped my head and sheepishly walked back toward the building with Will just a step behind.

"Ms. Garrison, Mr. Maddox," he called after us. "Tell your teachers I said your tardies are excused."

Chapter 9:
A Warning

We don't know who you think you are. But anyone who lives in this hell hole isn't worthy of Bridgeton. Do what we say or you're gonna pay. - The Bitch Brigade

I read the note over and over again. When I closed my eyes to blink away the tears of frustration and anger, I still saw the words as if they were engraved inside my eyelids. No matter what I did, or how hard I worked I'd still be the unworthy, poor black girl from Venton Heights. I snatched the note off of the door and stuffed it into my dance bag before entering my apartment.

"What's wrong?" my mother asked as she stirred a pot of what smelled like spaghetti sauce.

"Nothing. I'm fine." I dried my eyes on my sleeve and swallowed my emotion. I didn't want to worry my mother. I sat down at the kitchen table hoping to spend a few minutes talking to her. I barely saw her anymore. When Sasha and I were little and we lived in the little white house with the red shutters, we all used to be so close. My mom only worked during the day and she would always be home in time to pick us up from school and take us to the library or to a museum. So even if I'd had a bad day at school, I could always look forward to going home. I was always part of something. I belonged to a family.

"Well, I made some spaghetti for you and Sasha. I gotta get to work." My mother put the lid on the spaghetti sauce and whipped off her apron revealing her nurse's uniform.

"Mom, do you ever feel like you just don't belong?"

"Oh, Baby girl, are you getting picked on at school again?" She looked at her watch. "I really gotta get out of here. My shift starts at seven and I still have to catch a bus across town. Just tell Sasha who's bothering you. I'm sure she'll take care of it."

My mother grabbed her purse and kissed me on the cheek before dashing out of the door leaving me alone.

I went to my room and turned on Mozart's symphony number 25 in G minor in order to drown out the ghetto symphony of gunshots and sirens. I strapped on my pointe shoes and practiced my échappés and bourees to Mozart's stirring string composition while trying to stamp out thoughts of the Bitch Brigade. Dance was my way out. Ten years from now, when I'm dancing for the Russian Ballet, I'm not even going to remember those bitches. What did it matter what they thought of me?

I felt my courage rise along with the crescendo of the music. Who cared about them? The fact that I lived in this hell-hole and I went to bed to the sound of gun shots and police sirens actually made me stronger in some sense. If I could grow up in this place and not end up dead or pregnant by sixteen, I think I could handle a little second grade-like threat from a couple of blond bimbos. I grabbed the note out of my bag, crumpled it up, and tossed it into the trash.

Already feeling a bit relieved, I sat down to watch a video of Natalia Karleskaya with the Russian Ballet. As I watched, however, my mind kept wandering back to the note. I had been invisible at Bridgeton for two years. Most people didn't even know my name. So why did I suddenly become a target? It must have been because of Will. That was the only explanation.

And what exactly would they do to me? Name a cow after me? Big deal. Revealing where I lived would be embarrassing, but I'd get over it. It would actually affect Sasha more than me. So I had nothing to fear, right? But for some reason, a sickening sense of dread plopped in my stomach and grew at an alarming pace.

My thoughts drifted to that girl in the stairwell. What if that was the result of a Bitch Brigade threat? And what about the sudden rash of honor trials? What if the Bitch Brigade had somehow caused those too? Something told me these bitches were responsible for much worse things than Fat Tuesday cows. It was about time I figured out what these girls were really up to.

I didn't know exactly where to start my little investigation. Since I didn't have any friends at school, I didn't really feel comfortable walking up to a virtual stranger and asking if they knew any bitches. I guess I could have asked Will, but our...relationship, if I could call it that, was still pretty new. That would've been a pretty bizarre question.

That left Sasha.

"How much do you know about this Bitch Brigade?" I asked her while we ate lunch at our tree on the West Lawn.

"Why do you want to know?" She didn't even look up from her planner.

"Well, the cow incident was pretty mean and I'm starting to think they had something to do with a naked girl I found in a stairwell."

Sasha's head snapped up. "What?"

"That didn't come out right." I briefly explained what I knew about Emmaline Graham. When I finished, she returned her attention to her day planner. How could she seem so unconcerned? "Plus, I found a note from them on our apartment door."

She looked up again. "In Venton Heights?"

"Do we have another apartment?"

Sasha slammed her planner shut. "I have to go."

"But you said you would tell me about them. I feel I

should know the people threatening me. I need to know what I'm up against."

"I'll take care of it. Don't worry about it. But you should really stop asking questions, especially about Emmaline." Sasha crammed her barely touched food into a trash bag.

"So it was them, huh?"

Sasha didn't respond, but I could tell by the way she bit her bottom lip that I was right.

"And you know who they are, don't you? How can you let them get away with this?" I asked.

"Sonya, it's a little more complicated than that. Trust me, you just need to stay out of it. For your own good, no, for *our* own good, just stay out of it.

Chapter 10:
Cherry Picker

I tried to take Sasha's advice and ignore the possible danger of the Bitch Brigade. I knew Sasha could handle the situation. She'd take care of them the same way she did LaPorscha. I had nothing to worry about. So why was I still so worried?

The only thing that got my mind off the Bitch Brigade was spending time with Will. And we spent a lot of time together. Most mornings Will would meet me at the studio with flowers and a bagel and then help me clean. Some mornings, though, he was mysteriously absent. On those days, he'd meet me outside of my chemistry class with a single white flower. Then he'd apologize for being late, saying he'd had to press snooze three times. Then after school he'd meet me at the dance studio after basketball practice so we could have dinner together. And if he was late to that, he'd say it was because he had to shower three times. Hmph.

I wonder if those were just excuses. Maybe he had another girl on the side.

Anyway, when he wasn't mysteriously missing or being weirdly obsessed with the number three Will was really fun to hang out with and I knew he felt the same about me. In fact, he had even started calling me Sony, saying I was more entertaining than his Sony Playstation. I looked forward to spending time with him even though it counteracted my desire for invisibility. People noticed me when I was with Will and that was not a good thing.

"So, has he drilled you with his power tool yet?" a girl said to me in a low threatening voice as I loaded my books into my locker one morning. I was so tired from cleaning the studio that at first I couldn't register who the girl was. Then it struck me. Ashley Carter, a pretty blonde senior. I only knew her name because she often helped Lauren DeHaven with her numerous charitable events.

I didn't quite understand why she was talking to me about power tools, but then I figured out the innuendo. She was referring to Will. Instead of responding, I concentrated on my books and tried to ignore her. "You know that's the only reason he's with you, right?" she added.

I didn't respond.

"He's a top Cherry Picker you know. He gets extra points for virgins. And since you're like the last virgin on the planet he's gonna pick you." I tried to turn my back to her, but she continued. "He's a Panty Pirate. All he wants is the booty."

Her voice was so soft yet antagonizing. Only I could

hear her. And she had this sweet innocent expression on her face that completely contradicted the vicious vitriol that spewed from her mouth. "You don't believe me? Read this."

She stuffed a piece of paper in my hand. I slammed my locker shut and swung my backpack over my shoulder. In the process, though, I accidently smacked Ashley in the stomach. She stumbled back a few steps then yelled, "You hit me. I can't believe you hit me. Did you see that? She attacked me." Then some fake tears leaked out of her eyes. She should've won an Oscar. A few students ran to her aid and patted her on the back.

"Oh, come on. It was an accident," I tried to explain, but my years of practicing invisibility had worked too well. No one recognized my existence when precious Ashley Carter was in distress. I just melted into the background then skulked away.

Class was pretty pointless that day. I couldn't get my mind off of what Ashley had said. Will was a top Cherry Picker? What the heck did that mean? Well, I could imagine what it meant, but I didn't really want to. That couldn't be why he was with me. I mean we had been seeing each other for almost two weeks and he hadn't even kissed me. I'd been dreaming of that kiss. It would be my first.

I was sixteen and I'd never kissed a boy. I'd never had the opportunity. Boys in Venton Heights never seemed interested in me for some reason or maybe I'd never had the time to notice. Since I was eight years old, most of my time was spent dancing. Stefan and Sean were the only two male dancers my age at Ms. Alexander's studio. They were twins and I wasn't attracted to them in any way, shape, or form.

Most of the time I couldn't even tell them apart.

For over a year I had imagined my first kiss going to David Winthrop, but in the past two weeks, I looked forward to giving that honor to Will. Now I had doubts. Maybe Will wasn't for me.

I took out the sheet of paper Ashley had handed to me and read it while concealing it with my Spanish book. It was a copy of what looked like a score sheet for the Cherry Picker game. Will's name was in the top corner above a list of girl's names with a description of the sex act followed by the number of points awarded. My eyes watered and my lungs constricted as I read in lurid detail the things Will had done to or with other girls. Oral sex on a roller coaster, a threesome in his neighbor's hot tub, a virgin in a supermarket bathroom. I wanted to vomit. Was this the type of boy I was with?

My suspicions of Will possibly having another girl were starting to make sense. That's why he was always late. Maybe he was with other girls to keep his points up in the Cherry Picker game while he warmed me up in order to score super, mega, bonus points or something.

I closed my eyes and shook my head. There was no need to cry. Deep down I knew that wasn't true. The Will Maddox I'd gotten to know over the past two weeks wasn't using me for points. So why was my heartbeat accelerating making it hard for me to catch my breath? I couldn't figure out what bothered me so much. I mean, I already knew Will was promiscuous. The first two times I ever laid eyes on him, he'd just finished having sex in a public place. That wasn't the problem. It was in the past and I knew he really didn't want to be that person. That's why he told me he didn't like himself. This boy who brought me flowers at every opportunity for the past two and a half weeks did not want to be a cherry picking power tool anymore.

But, on the other hand, it had *only* been two weeks. Who's to say that in two more weeks he wouldn't lapse into old habits once again? How many times did my father say he'd change? And how many years had things stayed exactly the same until my mother finally got tired of it and kicked him out? I didn't want a life like that.

Ashley's revelation of the Cherry Picker game didn't make me doubt Will's intentions. I knew he wanted to change. The question was, could he?

Chapter 11:
The Championship

"You miss class? What you mean you miss class? You sick?" Ms. Alexander asked as she felt my head. Sasha and I stopped by the studio on the way to Will's Championship game. Sasha didn't feel I needed to explain my absence to Ms. Alexander, but I knew I couldn't just not show up without letting her know. She would think I was hit by a bus or something. I hadn't missed a dance class since I was ten-years-old with the chicken pox. I actually tried to go to class and she sent me home so as not to infect the other dancers.

"No, I'm not sick."

"No sick, no miss class. Get dressed." Ms. Alexander turned her attention back to the sound system and started flipping through CD's.

I really wanted to see Will play. But I couldn't lie to Ms. Alexander. I felt trapped. I stared at her for a few minutes trying to think of something to say. Finally, I resigned myself to the fact that I had to attend my pas de deux rehearsal.

I turned to go get changed when Sasha stepped in and said, "Ms. Alexander, I'm so sorry to disturb you, but our mother was in a horrible car accident just this morning. We've been by her side in the hospital all day. My sister is so committed to your dance program that she felt it absolutely necessary to tell you in person she couldn't attend and would rather be with our mother in her time of need."

"That true?" Ms. Alexander asked me. I started nodding furiously after Sasha pinched me hard in the back. "Why you no say that? Get out, go." She shooed us out with both hands.

"Oh, thank you for your understanding, Ms. Alexander," Sasha said graciously as a solitary tear streamed down her face. I stared at her in disbelief.

"Oh, don't give me that look," she said once we were outside. "You want to see Will don't you?"

"Yeah, but I didn't want to lie. What if she finds out?"

"So what if she does. How many of your weekends have you given that woman? You deserve a night for yourself once in a while. Besides, it's *Will Maddox*. You can't pass that up."

She was right. I couldn't pass it up. I really wanted to

get closer to him. I wanted to learn what drove him as a person. I wanted to figure out if he'd be strong enough to overcome the sex fiend personality he'd created for himself. Though we saw each other every day, I still didn't know a lot about him personally. Oddly enough, our conversations mostly revolved around opera music and fantasy basketball.

Even without him saying so specifically, I knew he had some pretty strange quirks. For instance, he always kept three green apple jolly ranchers in his left pocket, he always separated his food into three sections, he always wore the same "lucky" beat up red Converse All-Stars, he always carried his "lucky" basketball on Mondays, Wednesdays and Fridays and if I ever asked him to turn a light off in a room, he always had to flip the switch three times instead of just once. His habits didn't bother me so much as they intrigued me. But I didn't feel comfortable asking him about them yet. I wanted to get to know him better and making the effort to see him play in the championship was an important step.

When the teams came out to warm up, Will looked around in the crowd until he saw me. He gave me a nod of the head then shot the ball from really far away and it went in. He smiled at me as if to say 'that was for you.' I couldn't help but grin. Sasha noticed it too.

"Aren't you glad you came?" she said into my ear.

I really didn't understand a lot of the game, but I did understand that Will was really good. He was really, really good. I mean almost every time he shot the ball, it went in. And he shot it from really far away. And the people on the other team must have realized it too because they kept knocking him over and hitting him and stuff. Will just picked himself up with a smile and took his free shots which also always went in. I could see how happy playing basketball made him.

One time, however, they knocked him down and he didn't get up with a smile. The score was Bridgeton 77, other guys 72 in the fourth quarter with three minutes to go. Will stepped under the basket trying to get the ball when this obnoxious thug purposely elbowed him in the nose. Will went down with a thud and rolled around on his back clutching his face. I bolted out of my seat along with most of the audience trying to see if he was alright.

"Hey, that's not fair," I yelled. "Sasha, are they gonna just let that guy get away with that?"

"No, that's a flagrant foul. He'll get ejected," she said. I wanted to ask her to explain a flagrant foul, but I was too busy watching Will writhe in pain. He held his nose with both hands as blood seeped through his fingers. I felt my face flush with anger at his attacker and I felt the pain of his possibly broken nose. I blinked my tears away.

One of the other Bridgeton players lunged at the barbarian who attacked Will and within seconds, several players exchanged blows. Referees and coaches stormed the court trying to separate the boys. The crowd went insane.

It took twenty minutes to calm the boys down enough to resume the game. Six players were ejected and sent to the locker room. Even though Will didn't throw any punches, he also went to the locker room because the bleeding wouldn't stop.

Time ticked on and Will didn't emerge from the

locker room. I worried not only about his well being, but also about the score. With two minutes left, Bridgeton was down by two points. The team needed him. The crowd chanted his last name. Maddox, Maddox, Maddox. But still he didn't come out. I thought we were doomed. Bridgeton was down by five points with 57 seconds left. Finally, when the clock read 39 seconds Will emerged from the locker room and immediately joined his floundering team on the court. I thought there was no way Bridgeton could possible come back with only 39 seconds, but, then again, I had never been to a basketball game before.

Will reminded me of Vaslov Lopokova of the Russian Ballet the way he covered the court with style, grace, and expertise. I never knew basketball could be so beautiful. When the other team had the ball, Will waved his arms in their face trying to steal it. Then suddenly, he snatched the ball away from an opposing player and made a mad dash in the other direction. He stopped short, shot the ball and it went in. Three points. Then the other team had the ball again.

"Why are they taking so long? Why are they moving so slowly?" I asked Sasha.

"They're trying to run out the clock," she said, enthralled with the action and annoyed with my ignorance. The clock continued to click, five seconds, four seconds, three seconds. And that annoying team just kept passing the ball back and forth, back and forth. Then, with two seconds left, Will came out of nowhere and snatched the ball out of the air as someone on the other team tried to pass it. The crowd went insane. Will barely dribbled once before he flung the ball nearly from half court as the buzzer rang. I think my heart stopped as the ball slammed against the backboard then bounced on the rim. But it started up again as soon as the ball fell in. Three points. Bridgeton won its first state championship in 18 years. Caught up with emotion and excitement, I stormed the court along with the rest of the Bridgeton Academy population.

All the Bridgeton students began a spontaneous rendition of the school fight song. I didn't know the words so I just weaved through the crowd in search of Will. I wanted to congratulate him on his victory, but he was nowhere to be found. Disappointed, I found Sasha and told her I wanted to go home. But she said, "Don't be ridiculous. The captain is throwing a victory party. You have to go. I guarantee he'll be there."

So I went to the party and walked around aimlessly for over an hour feeling extremely uncomfortable. I didn't know anyone there and Sasha disappeared twenty seconds after we arrived. I wandered into some sort of showroom inside the huge house and studied the artwork displayed. I wasn't a huge fan of art, but I did recognize some of the pieces and the quiet of the room really eased the headache the loud revelries of my drunken classmates had caused.

"Cool, I've been there," I said to no one at all as I picked up a book with the Louvre on the cover.

"You have? I thought you went to Spain. You were in France too?" Will said as he stepped up behind me.

I spun around so quickly that I actually lost my balance for a second. Will grabbed my elbow and steadied me.

"Um, while I was in Barcelona at the dance festival, some of us dancers went to Paris one weekend and did the tourist thing."

"I still can't believe you've danced in Europe. I've never met anyone who ever did something that...amazing."

"You're pretty amazing yourself. That was a great game. I guess your shoes *are* lucky."

"I don't think it was the shoes. I think it was you." Will smiled at me. "Here, this is for you," he said, handing me the basketball that had been tucked under his arm. It's the game ball. I want you to have it."

I accepted the ball and turned it over in my hands. On it he'd written the words 'Will and Sonya.' I was so touched my heart sashayed in my chest. "What no flowers?" I asked jokingly.

Will unraveled a devilish grin. "How dare you doubt me?" He opened his jacket and pulled out three white tulips. As he handed them to me, he leaned over and kissed me on the cheek. His lips lingered there. The ball slipped from my hands and bounced away. His arms wrapped around my waist as his lips brushed against my chin then down to my neck. A rush of heat filled me. His lips felt so good on my body. I had to admit that a part of me, a big part of me, really wanted him. I not only wanted Will to be my first kiss, I wanted him to be my first everything. But another big part of me couldn't get his Cherry Picking out of my head. Before I gave my heart to him, I needed to hear everything…in his own words. I needed him to tell me who he was and who he wanted to be. Of course, there was no assurance that he'd always be true to me, but at least I wouldn't be going in blind.

He had started kissing up my neck, sensually searching for my lips when I blurted, "Will, are you a top Cherry Picker?"

Will stopped abruptly and sighed, letting his head fall on my shoulder. Then he stood up straight and turned away from me. "Who told you about that? Was it Makenzie?"

"Who?"

"Closet Girl I guess you can call her." When I shook my head, he said, "Let me think, it must have been Ashley then." Will sat on the couch and leaned his head back, staring up at the ceiling. "Cherry Picker is a game some of the jocks made up. We earn points for different sexual acts."

I wasn't going to let him off that easy. "What kind of acts?"

He sighed again. "Are you sure you want to hear about this?"

I nodded.

He took a deep breath and ran his fingers through his hair. "Well, sex in a closet is more points than sex in a bedroom because of the risk of being caught. The more dangerous the location, the more points. You get triple points for a threesome and things like that."

"What about the girl?"

"What do you mean?"

"Do you get more points for certain girls? Like virgins?"

Will bolted upright. "Do you think that's why I'm with you? Is that what Ashley told you?"

I nodded. "She showed me your score sheet."

"That bitch!" He kicked the coffee table. I didn't understand how he could let someone punch him in the nose on the basketball court and not show any signs of anger, yet Ashley telling me about Cherry Picker totally set him off. He was right though. It was a pretty bitchy thing to do. Could Ashley be a member of the Bitch Brigade?

Will closed his eyes and took a deep breath. "If you check the dates on that score sheet, you'll see that I haven't…added any points in over a month." He opened his eyes and looked directly at me as he said, "Sony, I've been with you for like two weeks and I haven't even kissed you. Does it seem like I'm using you for sex?"

"No." My voice was small and unsure. "I know, at least I hope, you're not using me. I think you honestly *think* you like me. I'm just afraid of what will happen when you get tired of me and you're ready to move on."

"Come here," he said patting the spot next to him on the couch. After I sat down, he wrapped his arm around me and kissed the side of my head. "I've done a lot of things I regret. I told you when we first met that I didn't like myself." He pulled me tighter. "You have no reason to believe me. You have no reason to trust me. I'll understand if you think I'm completely disgusting and you never want to see me again. But talking to you, spending time with you, just being near you makes me the happiest I've been in…in a really long time. Please don't give up on me. Just give me a chance."

I lost track of time as we sat in a warm embrace. I closed my eyes and blocked Ashley out of my mind and concentrated only on Will. I couldn't give up on him. In the short time I'd known him, I'd grown so close to him. Already, I felt he was a part of me.

Finally, Will said, "Come on, I'll take you home."

Here we go again. He wanted to take me home. How was I going to get out of it this time? "That's okay, Will. I'm here with Sasha. We'll get home together."

"How?"

We usually got Des to drop us off at a bus stop, but I didn't want to tell him that. So I just said, "Des."

"Oh, so you'll let him take you home, but not me? I'm insulted." Will pretended to be angry, but a smile hid behind his eyes.

I tried to come up with a quick retort, but nothing came to mind. The cold fingers of panic tickled my spine.

"Actually, I'm not going home. I'm going to the studio," I lied.

"Now? It's almost ten o'clock at night."

"Yeah, I need to print something out for my next audition. It's…really important."

Will shrugged. "Fine, I'll take you to the studio." He grabbed my hand and helped me off the couch.

"Okay." At least that would buy me some time to

figure out my next lie. There was no way I could let him see Venton Heights. "I should tell Sasha I'm leaving," I said as he led me out of the room. Maybe she'd help me figure out a way to keep Will away from Venton Heights.

Will held my hand as he led me through the house while we looked for Sasha.

"Do you want something to drink?" he asked as we walked through the kitchen. I looked around and saw nothing but beer and liquor bottles.

"I don't drink alcohol," I said regretting the words as soon as they'd left my mouth. What kind of high school girl didn't drink?

"I know you don't. You're not that kind of girl. And I'm glad. I don't drink either."

"Really?"

"Don't sound so surprised. I never drink. Ever." Will looked around the kitchen. "There has to be something non-alcoholic here."

"What about this punch?" I let go of his hand and scooped out some red liquid into a cup.

"Um, I doubt if that's non-alcoholic." Will gently took the cup out of my hand. "At a party, never drink anything you haven't seen poured out of a previously factory sealed container." I thought he was joking so I laughed a little, but then I noted the ominous look on his face. His eyes changed to a dark mysterious blue as if he knew from experience.

"Okay," I said, retreating from the cup. Will looked in the refrigerator and found an unopened can of Coke which he handed to me.

"I don't think we're gonna find your sister," he said as we circled the house for the third time.

"Yeah, I think you're right. I'm not worried though. She's probably just with Des."

"Well, let's head out before it gets too late. Wait a minute. We left your ball. I'll get it." Will scampered away leaving me by the refrigerator holding my Coke with both hands like a two year old holding a sippy cup. Then someone hugged me from behind and said, "There you are, Darling. I've been looking everywhere for you." I spun around and found myself being groped by Desmond.

"Sorry, Des, wrong sister," I said, twisting out of his arms.

"I'm sorry, I'm so sorry. I didn't realize how much you look like Sasha, especially from behind. Oh, not that I'm looking at your behind. It's your hair, you never wear your hair down."

Desmond continued blubbering his awkward profuse apology until I said, "It's fine, Des. So you don't know where Sasha is either? I've been looking for her too."

"She probably drove some intoxicated students home. She does that sometimes. Will you have her call my cell when you see her?" It struck me the way he said 'intoxicated students'. What high school kid talks that way? He was so proper it was ridiculous. He was like an accountant hiding in a teenager's body. I wondered what Sasha saw in him besides his money and his great car. But then again, with her proclivity for perfection, they were an excellent match.

"Why is she avoiding me?" I heard a voice say after Des had wandered off. I turned around and found Colbert staring at me. She looked a lot less like Eloise or Madeline or whichever one I was thinking of now that she was not in her uniform.

"Who?"

"Your sister." Colbert gave me her patented "duh" look, which Sasha had also adopted. I shrugged, not knowing what she was talking about. "Has she told you anything? What is she up to?" I shrugged again. Colbert twisted her lips and eyed me skeptically. "Look, just tell her...it didn't mean anything. Tell her...it's not like I'm in love with him or anything. And tell her..." Colbert bit her bottom lip and shifted her eyes then said, "Just tell her I'm sorry." Then she scampered away.

Sorry for what?

Chapter 12:
First Kiss

"So tell me about dancing in Spain," Will said once we were in his car.

"Well, a few years ago Ms. Alexander told me about this festival that takes place every six years in Barcelona. It's extremely prestigious. Dancers from all over the world come and take part and offer master classes and even give personal critiques of some of your work. I worked for months on my audition pieces. One of my numbers was an exact replica of Natalia Karleskaya's solo to a Shostakovich concerto. They not only accepted me to the festival, but I received a personal note from Natalia saying she enjoyed my rendition of her solo and then she gave me some suggestions on how I could make it better. Can you believe that? Isn't that amazing? That's like Michael Jordan writing you and telling you how you can improve that loop up shot thing that you do."

Will laughed and said, "It's called a lay-up, and I'm

surprised you know who Michael Jordan is."

"Of course I do, he's like the Baryshnikov of basketball. Anyway, I was so excited I spent the next two months completely obsessed with the Spanish language. I wanted to be able to speak at least a little before I got there. By the end of the summer, I was fluent." I continued talking non-stop about everything I'd done while I was in Europe; the dancers I met, the performances I saw, the museums I went to. Before I knew it forty-five minutes had passed and we were sitting in front of the studio. Will was so easy to talk to. I don't think I'd told anyone so many details of my trip to Spain. Not even Sasha.

"Well, thanks for the ride, Will." I hoped to just jump out of the car and wave goodbye, but it wasn't going to be so easy to get rid of him. "What are you doing?" I asked when he opened his door.

"You didn't think I was going to leave you here by yourself this late at night, did you?" He smiled and instantly melted away my defenses. "Why don't you show me your audition piece?"

Will came around and opened my door for me. My mind raced as I tried to think of a way to get rid of him. I had to give him points for persistence. He certainly wasn't one to give up easily. He seemed downright determined to see where I lived. Deep down I knew I was overreacting. Really all he wanted was to make sure I got home safely. He was being sweet and showing how much he cared about me.

I stepped out of the car and said, "Actually, I have three audition pieces. I'm supposed to showcase different styles and different technical strengths. But I'm not done with the choreography. How about I show you when I'm finished?" Will shrugged not picking up on my tone of dismissal. He stood on the sidewalk waiting for me to unlock the door to the studio. "I'm fine here, Will. I can get home on my own. It's not far."

"You're only gonna be a few minutes, right? I can wait." He jammed his hands in his pocket and rocked on his heels. I sighed and went to open the door.

After we entered the studio, I led him to Ms. Alexander's office and sat at her computer. I didn't need another copy of my application, but I printed one anyway. I had to do something to make the trip seem worthwhile.

"What are you auditioning for this time?" he asked as he walked around Ms. Alexander's office.

"It's a festival in Rome. If I play my cards right, I could also get accepted to their academic program and do my senior year of school there. I've already started working on my Italian." I cleared my throat and in my best Italian accent said, "*Scusi, dov'e la toilette?*" Will smiled as he looked at my wall of achievements. One side of Ms. Alexander's office was covered with awards, photographs, and performance programs she had kept to show off my accomplishments. It was like a little shrine to me.

"Look at all these awards you've got. Why don't you keep these at home?"

"This place is more my home than my home is. If that makes any sense."

"Yeah, it makes perfect sense, actually. My home really isn't a home either." That was an interesting piece of information. Maybe that was why his eyes were sad. He didn't have a happy home life. I hoped he'd tell me more.

"What do you mean?" I asked. Will looked at me. I could tell he mentally debated whether he wanted to share something or not. He suddenly had this emotionally crushed expression on his face.

"Two years ago, both my parents were killed by a drunk driver on their way home from one of my basketball games." My mouth flew open. An ambush of tears gathered behind my eyes.

"The driver was 16. He went to school with me. He was leaving one party and was on his way to another." Will paused for a moment. I wasn't sure if he was going to continue or not as he just stared at the wall like he was looking through it. "I had to leave everything and everyone I knew in Chicago and move in with my older sister, Julia, here in New Jersey," he continued after a few moments. I didn't know what to say as Will touched some of the awards on the wall wistfully. "What's worse is that she's an alcoholic, so every day I get to watch her slowly kill herself. Alcohol took my parents and now it's taking my sister. That's why I don't drink. Ever."

My heart ached for Will. I wanted to say something to erase his pain, but I couldn't come up with anything. I stood up from the computer and walked over to him. I embraced him and held him for a long time. Then we sat down on Ms. Alexander's couch.

"It hurts so much sometimes to go out on the court

and not see them in the crowd cheering for me." Two tears streamed down his face. Will wiped them away frantically with the inside of his sleeve. "I can't believe I'm crying in front of you. You must think I'm some kind of wimp," he sniffled, trying to regain his composure.

"Actually, I think you're pretty brave for telling me all this." At that moment, he was the bravest person I knew. He spilled his guts to me about something so devastatingly personal, and I was afraid to let him find out I lived in Venton Heights. How shallow could I be?

"You're crying, too," he said, brushing a tear away from my face with his fingertips.

"Am I? I didn't realize. I just hate to see people in pain."

"I can tell. That's why I trust you so much. I haven't told anyone here about my family. But there's something special about you. I knew it the first time I saw you."

"You mean when you attacked me with a door?"

Will smiled. "Yeah. That day changed my life. I couldn't get you out of my head. You gave me something to think about besides my own misery. For so long I was afraid to talk to you in person, because I thought there was no way you could live up to what I had built you up to be in my mind." Will stared at me with eyes more intense than a Wagner overture. I could tell he wanted to kiss me.

"Well, how am I doing?" I asked. "Am I living up to what you built me up to be in your mind?"

Will smiled that smile that melted away all my inhibitions, all my insecurities, all my doubts, hell, it melted my brain at that point as he said, "You're so much better than anything I could have imagined." Then he pressed his soft sweet lips to mine and swept me up into a place I'd never been before. I felt hot and lightheaded and giddy, kind of like how I feel after I nail the turn sequence from Swan Lake in front of a sold out audience, except there was an added sensation; some electric thrill pierced through me that I'd never felt from ballet.

At first, the kiss tantalized my senses like a delicate caress, but then he dove deeper. Our lips parted simultaneously and our tongues began a dance choreographed by pure passion. It didn't matter that I had never kissed anyone before and I had no idea what I was doing because he knew exactly what to do. He knew exactly where to place his tongue so as to massage the tension out of mine. He knew exactly how to place his gentle hand on the small of my back so as to make even my toes tingle. And when he moved his lips away from my mouth and nuzzled my neck I could feel my back involuntarily arch and my breasts press against his muscular chest.

I lost myself in his kisses and his hands all over my body. But suddenly, he stopped.

"What? What's wrong?" I asked in a panic.

"Nothing's wrong. I just think we should stop now."

"Why? Oh God, am I a bad kisser?" How humiliating. I bet he could tell that I'd never kissed a guy before and thought I was horrible at it.

"No, God no. You're...you're amazing." Will stood and walked to the other side of the room as if he had to put distance between us. "It's me. I'm the problem. I'm a human cancer, Sonya. I'm an awful person who ruins lives. I don't want to do that to you."

"Will, don't say that -"

"Why not? It's true." He crossed his arms and leaned against the wall. "Do you know why I always bring you white flowers?" I shook my head. "Because they symbolize innocence, purity, and beauty and that's what you mean to me. I don't want to ruin that."

Chapter 13:
Angel

It took a full hour to convince Will to let me walk home by myself. I felt kind of silly still hiding where I lived after he had revealed so much to me, but I'd made a promise to Sasha long before I met him. I couldn't break that promise to her. She worked so hard to create a certain image and reputation for herself at Bridgeton. Who was I to come along and shatter that? Although I knew in my heart I could trust Will, it wouldn't have mattered to Sasha. She would've just seen it as a betrayal of trust.

"Will, please, I'll be fine. I have a can of mace and I'll call you as soon as I get in the door. I walk home alone all the time."

He sighed, tiring of the debate we'd been having, and said, "If I don't hear from you in exactly 25 minutes, I'm calling the police and coming to look for you myself."

He gave me a long kiss then rested his forehead against mine. He slowly let me out of his embrace then murmured, "I can't believe I'm letting you do this," while getting into his BMW.

I literally had to run and take several short cuts through people's backyards in order to make it from Ms. Alexander's studio to Venton Heights in 25 minutes. But I made it with three minutes to spare. When I entered the apartment, I noticed my mother had collapsed on the living room couch. She must've been completely exhausted to be sleeping on that couch. That couch grossed me out. We found it on the side of the road after it had been rained on. Although we cleaned it and dried it, it was still, well, crunchy for lack of a better word.

My mother hadn't even taken off her nursing shoes. She was catching a few minutes of well-needed rest before she woke up at the crack of dawn to go to her other job.

I went into the bedroom Sasha and I shared and found she too had collapsed from exhaustion. My sister, still fully dressed, had fallen asleep in a Spanish book. Spanish was the only class we had together. I took Advanced Placement Spanish Literature because I spoke it fluently. I did pretty well in the class, too; sometimes even better than Sasha.

I couldn't believe my sister did homework on Saturday nights. We didn't even have any assignments due in the near future. Or, at least, I didn't remember getting a Post It about one. And the book she had wasn't even from our class. Hmm...strange, I thought. I went over to my bed and found a Post It on my pillow saying, "If I'm asleep, wake me up. We need to talk about Will."

Oh God, Will! I had to call him before he freaked out with worry and called the police. I borrowed Sasha's cell phone since our home phone had been cut off again and I went into my mother's bedroom.

Will and I talked well into the morning. After a few hours I knew just about everything about him. While he told me all about his mother the classical pianist, his father the college professor and his life in Chicago I was still too ashamed to tell him where I came from.

"Will, can I ask you a personal question?"

"You can ask me anything you want."

"When did you start seeing a psychiatrist?"

There was silence on the phone for a moment. "Are you sure you want to know?"

I nodded, then realized he couldn't see me through the phone so I said, "I'm sure."

He was silent again for so long I thought he wasn't going to answer. Finally he took a deep breath and said, "After my suicide attempt."

I gasped. The thought that he could be dead right now brought a rush of pain to my heart. What if we had never met? My throat tightened and warm tears dribbled down my cheeks as I tried to hold in my emotion.

"Sony? Are you crying?"

"No."

Will could tell from the quiver in my voice that I was lying. "I'm sorry. I shouldn't have told you that. I didn't mean to upset you."

"Don't apologize." I sniffled. "I just…I can't imagine what you've been through."

"I'm much better now. It's been almost a year since I took the pills. Please don't worry about me."

"Are you sure you're better?"

"Yeah, I'm sure. Why?"

"Well, it's just that I've noticed some strange -"

"Obsessive Compulsive Disorder." He interrupted me. "As hard as I try, I just can't avoid certain little rituals. If I don't eat my food in threes, for example, I literally get sick and vomit. The ticks get pretty embarrassing sometimes, but most people just assume I'm a run of the mill superstitious athlete. I'm actually much better than I used to be before I started seeing a therapist. My doctor says I'm still getting even better every day too. And since I've met you, the ticks have subsided even more."

"Really?"

"Yep, when I saw you dance in the Nutcracker last December it -"

"Wait. You saw me in the Nutcracker?"

"Yeah. I even sent you flowers. White orchids."

I remembered getting the flowers. They didn't have a

card so I just assumed they were from Sasha or Ms. Alexander.

"Anyway, when I sat through that performance, it was the first time in three months I went two straight hours without going to my car and tapping the door three times to make sure it was locked. You were so mesmerizing, I didn't…I couldn't leave the show. Now I can go six hours straight without the door tapping ritual. I'm finally getting a decent amount of sleep."

"Wow." I really couldn't think of anything else to say. For so long Will had hidden his wounded soul behind a false wall of strength and confidence. But he had let me in. I felt like I was the only in the world who had seen his vulnerability.

"You're like my angel," he said after a moment. "And if you don't mind, I think I just might fall in love with you."

Chapter 14:
Make it Take it

I don't even really remember falling asleep the night I talked on the phone with Will. But I do remember Sasha shaking me awake early the next morning.

"Leave me alone. What do you want?" I grumbled.

"You have to break up with Will," she said in a matter-of-fact tone.

I blinked my eyes open and stared at her. Had she lost her mind? "What are you talking about? Why?"

"You just do, okay? There's a lot you don't know about him. He's not good for you."

"Sasha, two weeks ago you nearly forced me to go out on a date with him. Now you want me to break up with him? What's gotten into you?" I sat up and rubbed the sleep out of my eyes.

Sasha chewed her bottom lip as if searching for what to say next. "Everyone saw you at the party last night."

"So? Isn't that what you wanted? Didn't you want me to improve my social status?"

"Everyone thinks you slept with him," she said, ignoring my questions. "You were alone in a room with him for almost an hour. I don't want people thinking my sister is a slut."

I was completely confused. "Two weeks ago," I began slowly as if speaking to a three-year-old, "you gave me a handful of condoms just for that purpose. Do you not remember this?"

"Yeah, well things are different now."

"What things?" I asked. She didn't respond. "Well, we didn't have sex if that's what you are concerned about. I don't care what everyone thinks."

"Do you know about Cherry Picker?" she asked still standing over me.

"Yes, he told me everything. And I don't care. He's not like that anymore."

"Of course he is. You think he changed in just two weeks? He's just using you for points."

I shook my head and sighed. I was too tired to argue with her. "I'm going back to sleep." I scooted back down under the covers and put the pillow over my head.

A few minutes later, she ripped the pillow away and

said, "Do you know he's crazy? He goes to a psychiatrist."

"Yes, I know he goes to a psychiatrist. And he's not crazy."

"Well then why does he go to a psychiatrist?"

I paused. I couldn't tell her about Will's family or his suicide attempt. I didn't want to betray his trust. I sat up again and decided to try and figure out what was really motivating Sasha's sudden change of attitude. "Sasha, what's really going on?"

She sat down on the bed. "It's Ashley, Brittany, and Lauren DeHaven. You've really pissed them off by dating Will."

"Are they the Bitch Brigade?"

She nodded sheepishly.

I shrugged. "So?"

"What do you mean 'so'? You have no idea what these bitches are capable of."

"Who cares?"

"I do. I care, Sonya. I've worked too hard for my reputation just to have it ruined because you're suddenly in love with a sex-crazed psycho."

"Don't call him that," I said through clenched teeth.

Sasha put her head in her hands. "Sis, I'm begging you. Just end it before something bad happens."

I sighed. "I can't. He needs me."

She looked up. "What about me? What about what *I* need?" Sasha hopped off the bed and stormed out the bedroom. I followed and caught her right before she opened the front door.

"Sasha, wait." She turned to look at me. I didn't quite know what to say. I didn't want her to leave angry at me, but she obviously wasn't in the mood for communication. I decided to change the subject. "Colbert wanted me to tell you something."

Sasha rolled her eyes. "What did *she* want?"

"Uh, let's see," I said, walking to the fridge while trying to recall as much of the message as I could. "She said it didn't mean anything, and she's not in love with him, and she's sorry. What does that mean?" I thought about the words for the first time. It kind of sounded like Colbert had slept with Sasha's boyfriend or something. "Did Colbert sleep with Desmond?" I asked. "Is that why you're so upset about Will and me?"

Sasha burst out laughing.

"Of course not. Desi would never cheat on me," she said when her laughter subsided. "Colbert is a very … disturbed girl," Sasha began seriously. "She's been making some bad decisions and I've been trying to warn her and she's not taking my advice. Sound familiar?" She raised an eyebrow to indicate she was referring to me.

That was odd. I never thought of Colbert as

disturbed. I always thought she and Sasha were a lot alike.

***

I realized I needed to find out more about the Bitch Brigade. They were becoming too much of an intrusion on my life. I just knew that somehow they were going to try to break up Will and me. Sasha seemed too afraid to tell me anymore about them. But my conversation with her reminded me of someone else who might be able to give me some answers.

"I gave Sasha your message," I said to Colbert outside her locker Monday morning. Besides me, Colbert was the closest person to Sasha. I was sure she would know at least as much as Sasha if not more.

"You did? What did she say?" Colbert shut her locker and stared at me with wide curious eyes.

"Nothing much really. Just -"

"Is she still mad at me?"

I shrugged. "No idea."

"Great, Sonya. You're a great help." She rolled her eyes.

"Sorry. I'll help you, I promise. But I need a little favor in return."

"What."

"Tell me about the Bitch Brigade."

"No way." Colbert turned away.

"Wait." I grabbed her shoulder and turned her around. Thankfully, she wasn't into theatrics like Ashley was. "Do you want to make up with Sasha or not? How important is my sister's friendship to you?"

Colbert sighed then looked around. The bell sounded and students started herding into classrooms. She grabbed my arm then pulled me into the same stairwell where I found Emmaline.

"Okay, what do you already know?" she asked once we were alone.

"I know they're behind the Fat Tuesday prank. I suspect they stripped Emmaline and left her naked right here in this stairwell. They left a threatening note on my door. Now Sasha says Ashley, Brittany, and Lauren are pissed that I'm dating Will."

"She gave you names?" Colbert's eyes expanded.

"Yeah, why?"

"Because no one really knows for sure who's in the Bitch Brigade. It's a secret society. You have to be invited in, then there's some sort of initiation and you're sworn to secrecy for life. Each year a new Queen Bitch is selected to run the society and then she passes on the power to an underclassman before she leaves. The Bitch Brigade has been talked about for longer than we've been alive. My mother remembers them from when she was here. In all that time, no member has been officially identified."

"Well Sasha knows who they are. Maybe that's the first step to bringing them down. You, me, and Sasha can stand up to them. Isn't it about time someone stopped them?"

Colbert stared at me as if I was speaking another language. I actually did a mental check to make sure I hadn't slipped into Spanish. Suddenly Colbert started laughing. Her shrill cackle filled the empty stairwell.

"Oh my God. I thought you were serious for a minute. Sonya, you can't stop them. They have too much power. Listen, my advice to you is to do whatever Sasha tells you. That's what I should've done." She closed her eyes and shook her head. She placed the back of her hand on her forehead as if she was about to swoon. I noticed her trembling fingers. "I am so not up for school today."

"Are you sick?"

Colbert rolled her eyes again. "Yeah, Sonya, I'm sick. In fact, I need to make a visit to Dr. Bloomingdale's." She dug her cell phone out of her pocket and said, "I'm out," while bounding down the stairs toward the first floor exit. "Don't forget to talk to Sasha for me." She called out behind her.

"Okay," I said even though I still wasn't quite sure what I was supposed to talk to her about.

***

"So where are we going?" I asked Will after school a few days later.

Will dribbled his lucky basketball on the sidewalk.

"We're gonna go improve your basketball skills."

"*Improve* my basketball skills? Mr. Maddox, that would imply I have some basketball skills to begin with. If that's what you think, you are sadly mistaken."

Will laughed. "Don't worry, I'm a good teacher." He tossed me his basketball. In true pathetic girl fashion, I yelped and stepped out of the way. He shook his head. "This is gonna be harder than I thought.

Thankfully, Bridgeton's gym was empty so no one could see my pitiful attempts at imitating Will's moves. After about thirty minutes of learning some basics and throwing up some practice shots that never went in, Will decided to challenge me.

"We're gonna play a game of Make-it Take-it."

"Okay, how do you play?" I asked, clapping my hands together and doing my best imitation of an excited, pumped jock.

Will chuckled. "Well, usually, Make-it Take-it just means that if you make a shot you take possession of the ball. But I was thinking of adding a little twist to it." Will's trademark devilish grin returned. God, he was sexy.

"What did you have in mind?"

Will took the ball and spun it around on his index finger as he said, "Well, let's say I make a shot, then I get to take a kiss…anywhere I want."

My breath caught in my chest causing my heart to

momentarily pause. My skin tingled in anticipation. This was about to be one hot February afternoon.

Will tossed me the ball and let me take the first shot. He laughed when I lobbed it up and it slammed against the backboard. Then he came from out of nowhere, grabbed the rebound and sunk an easy lay-up. Smiling as if about to burst with delight, he strode over to me.

"Time to claim my prize."

I closed my eyes and lifted my head in expectation of his lips on mine. I felt his face nearing and smelled his green apple scented breath, but I didn't get what I was expecting. Instead, he lifted my hair and graced the side of my neck with his soft, powerful lips. He massaged the sensitive area with his tongue then pulled away abruptly, leaving me aching for more.

"That's one," he said, dribbling the ball around me. "We play to fifteen."

I didn't know if I could take fourteen more kisses like that. I already felt weak in the knees. Will kept dribbling and waiting for me to move.

"You plan on playing any defense?" he asked after a few seconds.

I snapped out of the momentary trance that kiss had put me in and tried to block Will's next shot. He toyed with me by dribbling the ball through his legs and around his back laughing the entire time. If he wasn't so darn cute and sexy, I might have gotten annoyed.

I tried to focus and keep my eyes on the ball, but seconds later he did some sort of turn and side step then sailed toward the basket almost making a slam dunk.

"Oh, now you're just showing off," I said, crossing my arms and feigning irritation.

Will just smiled and grabbed my hand. Then he pulled me toward him, slamming my body against his in the process. He wrapped his arms around my waist and stared into my eyes. He licked his lips slowly as he leaned down. His nose touched mine and his breath caressed my lips. He left me in that state of blissful agony while he rocked me back and forth in a sensual two-step. Finally, he lifted my chin to the left and stroked my right collar bone with a gentle kiss.

He smiled. "That's two."

Still woozy from the kiss, I tried to concentrate and figure out how to steal the ball. It didn't work. Within seconds he'd made another shot. This time when he approached me he let his fingers slowly trace the lines of my neck. Then he unbuttoned the top button of my uniform shirt. I tried to look down to see what he was doing, but he lifted my chin and held my eyes with his as he undid another button. The palm of his hand slid down to the swell of my breasts and my mind went fuzzy. The only thing I could think about was how much I wanted him to rip my shirt completely off. He was driving me crazy.

Will leaned down and kissed where his hand had just been, letting his tongue slip between my breasts. My whole body felt engulfed in flames.

"That's three," he said, pulling away.

I grabbed his shirt and pulled him back to me. "Where do you think you're going?" I slipped my hands under his untucked shirt letting my hands roam his smooth, rock hard chest.

"Hey, we have a game to finish," he teased as he removed my hands from his body and started dribbling again.

"Will," I whined.

"What?" he replied innocently.

I decided I'd had enough of this. When he squared up to take his next shot, I ran and jumped on his back, throwing him off balance. As he fell to the ground, I landed gracefully on my toes and easily retrieved the stray ball. I stood right under the basket and banked it off the backboard and into the net.

"See, you made it," he said, getting to his feet. "Told you I was a good teacher."

"Shut up and kiss me." I grabbed his shirt and pulled him to me. I moaned in ecstasy as the taste of his lips finally satisfied my intense craving. My arms reached for his neck. He lifted me off the ground and my legs wrapped around his waist.

His hands slid under my uniform skirt clutching and massaging my thighs all the way up to my panties. I pressed my body closer to his. I wanted to melt into his essence. I wanted to be one with him.

Leslie DuBois

Will knelt to the ground and laid me down on my back. He ripped open my shirt then rained luscious kisses on my breasts. He created a path with his tongue down to my navel then down to my skirt. In one swift movement, he whisked my skirt off. He kissed my stomach again as his thumbs hooked into the sides of my panties.

"I want you so bad," he said, slowly tugging my panties down.

"I want you too, Will. I want you to be my first. I want you to be my one and only."

Will froze. He sighed and rolled off of me. I knew what the problem was. "Will, it's okay. I'm ready. I want to do this."

He shook his head. "You don't want to know how many times I've had sex in this very gym and with how many girls. It makes me sick just thinking about it." He closed his eyes and shook his head again. "I want it to be different with you. I don't want to be Will the Drill with you." I scooted closer to him and rested my head on his chest. He rubbed my back and said, "*You* might be ready, Sonya, but *I'm* not."

"I understand." I tilted my head back and stared into his sweet yet tortured eyes.

"Isn't that weird? With you...when it means something...I'm afraid."

I shrugged. "I like weird."

Chapter 15:
What Matters

Will had ripped the buttons right off of my shirt so he let me wear his as we lay in each other's arms staring at the gym ceiling.

"Let's go to Prom together," he said.

"Prom?"

"Yeah, it's a little thing Bridgeton has every year where people dress up and dance."

I slapped him playfully on the stomach. "I know what Prom is. I just don't think it's my thing."

"Why not?" he asked.

"In case you haven't noticed, I don't really fit in here at Bridgeton."

Will shrugged. "So what?"

"I already feel out of place on a daily basis here at this school. I'd feel even more awkward at a thing like Prom. I don't even have the right clothes to wear. I just don't belong at something like that."

"I'll tell you where you belong. Right here, with me." He squeezed me tighter. "Why don't you let me buy you a dress?"

I leaned up on my elbow and stared at him. "What makes you think I need you to buy me a dress?" For some reason I was annoyed. Did he just assume I was too broke to buy my own dress? Of course, I was too poor. But he didn't know that. Or did he?

"What? No…I didn't mean anything…I just want to buy you a dress."

I thought about this for a second. Will was just being nice. I was seriously being paranoid.

"I'm not trying to say you're poor or anything," Will continued. "But, I mean, you do clean the dance studio in exchange for lessons don't you?"

"Dance studio?" I sat up and grabbed Will's arm to look at his watch. "Oh my God, I'm late for rehearsal. I gotta get to the studio." I jumped up and started gathering my things.

"Don't worry, I'll tell Ms. Alexander it was my fault," Will said, grabbing his keys.

"She won't care. She's gonna kill me."

I changed into my leotard and tights while Will sped down the highway that separated Bridgeton and my dance studio. Considering he had just seen me in my bra and panties, I found no need for modesty.

When we got there, I jumped out of the car and dashed inside to the main recital room. Rehearsal for the spring show was already in full swing. She hadn't waited for me. Cassie Odachowski was dancing my part. She was doing the choreography that Ms. Alexander had created with me in mind. And she looked good. This was bad.

As soon as Ms. Alexander noticed my presence, she stopped the music. "You late," she said, slamming her stick on the ground.

Will stepped into the classroom. "I apologize, Ms. Alexander. It was my fault."

"Who are you?" she snapped.

"I'm her boyfriend." I should've felt a sense of pride that someone as cute as Will was professing his allegiance to me in front of all my fellow dancers. But instead, I felt an overwhelming sense of dread. Like two important pieces of my life were colliding and setting things asunder.

"No boyfriends. Shoo!" she said, waving her stick at him. At first Will was too shocked to move. But then he turned on his heels and fled the studio for fear of being beaten up by a little old Japanese woman.

***

I couldn't get the sight of Cassie dancing my

choreography out of my head. Something like that had never happened to me before. I was the star of the dance studio. I was the one Ms. Alexander used to fill in for parts and demonstrate choreography. What was happening to me? Was I letting Will interfere too much with my career?

The next day my daydreaming about Will and dance led me to walk straight into Headmaster Collins. And I mean straight into him. My face firmly planted into his chest. With his formidable and solid shape, I thought for a moment that I had just walked into a wall...or a cow. But then he cracked his knuckles causing my skin to crawl. My plan to never have to speak directly to him again had failed.

"You're going the wrong way, young lady. There's an honor trial in Dardem Hall," he said as he put his hand on my shoulder and turned me around to walk in the same direction as him.

I remember the first time I met Headmaster Collins. It was two years ago during my interview to get into Bridgeton. He was the last stop after a day of meeting with teachers, taking entrance exams and performing my dance audition. He barely spoke the entire half an hour I sat in his office. He read my file while shaking his head disapprovingly and occasionally glancing at me from over the top of the folder. When he did speak he said, "Why do you belong at Bridgeton Academy?" I remember I had to concentrate in order to not lose control of my bodily functions. I knew he had looked at my grades and realized they paled in comparison to my sister's. I tried to think of some excuse for why I had performed so poorly in my previous classes and why I needed to be accepted to Bridgeton in order to improve. I thought about the beautiful campus I'd seen all day and dreaded heading back to Grover Cleveland High School. I thought of Sasha and how disappointed she'd be in me if I blew this interview and didn't get in. But for the life of me I couldn't think of anything to say that would convince him to let me into his school. So, I just pretended he wasn't sitting in front of me and said the first thing that came to my mind.

"I don't belong at Bridgeton. But, I also don't belong in Venton Heights. Have you heard of Venton Heights? It's an awful place to live and I wouldn't wish it on my worst enemy. Right now, in my life, the only time I belong is when I'm on stage performing. I know I'm not the smartest person in the world. But I think intelligence isn't only reflected in academics. True intelligence also encompasses experiences of successes and failures, it involves character, and the ability to use those qualities to make decisions in life. The ability to make the types of decisions that determine your true self. I guess what I'm trying to say is that I'm only fourteen and I still need to find out who I am. I need to 'find myself', for lack of a better analogy. Why not let Bridgeton be the place where I start looking?"

Something I said must have hit home because, after pausing, he looked me straight in the eye and said, "Welcome to Bridgeton."

Now walking down the hallway with his hand on my shoulder, I wondered if I'd lived up to his expectations.

"Ms. Garrison," he said right before we entered Dardem Hall, "if you don't mind, I'd like for you to talk with Emmaline Graham. Maybe you can convince her to come forward."

"Me? Why me?"

"You seem to have a positive effect on people. I've certainly noticed a change in Mr. Maddox." I blushed. Well, as much as a black girl can blush anyway. "Just think about it. I'll give you her address in case you decide to do it."

I was just about to tell him that I didn't think I could do it when he took his hand off my shoulder and cracked his knuckles making my skin crawl. Instead, I just ended up nodding and saying, "Yes, sir."

I entered Dardem Hall to find my regular seat. As usual, Will was already there waiting for me. Will always anticipated where I'd be and just appeared there. How did he do that? I guess it wasn't really that hard. If I wasn't at the studio, I was at school. At school, I could be found either in class, at the tree where Sasha and I ate lunch, or in Dardem Hall for a trial.

Will monopolized a lot of my time. Even if I wasn't with him, which wasn't very often, I thought about him. He distracted me way too much. Each day I caught more and more heat from Ms. Alexander. I knew I had to do something.

"You are magnificent dancer and beautiful girl. You can't throw away for first boy to look at you," Ms. Alexander said to me a week later after an especially bad pointe class. I actually ran into Elizabeth Weeks nearly injuring her. Ms. Alexander ended class early and pulled me into her office. She sat behind her desk and after sighing heavily she spoke slowly and clearly even adding in all of her prepositions and articles to make sure I understood everything over her accent.

"When you on stage you have to be focused. You could have hurt yourself and Elizabeth just now. Then where would I be? You are best dancer here. Sit," she said, pointing to the couch. The feel of the couch immediately brought back the sensation of Will's lips all over me. It took all of my mental faculties to purge Will's face from my thoughts and focus on the little Japanese figure lecturing me. "You have big audition soon. You can't dance for them the way you have danced for me lately." It seemed strange to me that she mentioned the audition, but didn't mention the spring show which was well before the audition. Had she already replaced me with Cassie?

"I'm sorry, Ms. Alexander. I know I can do better. I'm sorry. I'll concentrate. I promise." She looked at me skeptically and twisted her lips. "Please don't give my part to Cassie. I can do this. I know I can."

She sighed and said, "Fine, but no more boy!" I couldn't bring myself to tell Will he was no longer welcome at the studio. The next time he showed up, I had Ms. Alexander tell him he couldn't come back.

So, Will went off to play basketball nearby while I rehearsed and I actually found myself relieved. I felt like a jerk. I had this awesome, wonderful, caring boyfriend and I looked forward to time away from him.

The basketball court he found to play on was only a few blocks away from Venton Heights.

"Don't you feel uncomfortable playing basketball in that inner city neighborhood? It's a really bad neighborhood...so I've heard," I said to him while we ate dinner between my classes one evening.

"Why would I feel uncomfortable?"

I stared at him incredulously. Did he really not know? "Because you're rich and white and all the people there are poor and black."

"This," he said, spinning the ball on his index finger, "is a great equalizer. When I'm playing ball, race doesn't matter. Just like when I'm with you. Race doesn't matter." He placed the ball in his lap then grabbed my hand and stared into my eyes as if he knew something I didn't. "You know, I've met a lot of nice guys out there on the court. I don't care what neighborhood they sleep in at night, I still consider them my friends. They're not defined by where they live. No one is."

Hmph. That wasn't Sasha's opinion. According to her, life in Venton Heights was a death sentence. But as long as we kept the two worlds of Venton Heights and Bridgeton completely separate, we had a chance at escape.

Maybe race didn't matter to Will, but it mattered to other people. It mattered a lot.

Chapter 16:
Nowhere to Go

"Can I help you?" Will's sister asked when she opened the door. Actually, I just assumed it was his sister since we had never officially met. She looked just like Will except shorter and much, much older. Will told me she was 28 but she looked about 38. Maybe the alcohol abuse had aged her.

"Oh, I'm here for Will, I'm his…girlfriend." The word 'girlfriend' kind of got stuck in my throat. I had never used that word in reference to myself before.

I was so wrapped up in the word girlfriend that I almost didn't notice the change in Julia's face. She had opened the door with a pleasant smile, but as soon as I said the word 'girlfriend' her smile froze and her eyes bulged a little. I thought it was an odd reaction.

"Girlfriend?" she repeated with the same plastered smile. I nodded. "William!" she called, turning away from the door not even bothering to invite me in. "William Riley Maddox, may I talk to you please?"

I let myself in and took a seat on the couch. I looked at all the family portraits in the living room as I heard the muffled voices of Will and Julia from another room. As I picked up a picture of Will when he was probably about 9 years old, I thought about how different our worlds were at that time. He was living in a safe little cozy suburban home while I was being thrust into the ghetto. He probably came home every night to Stove Top stuffing and Little Debbie snack cakes while I ate saltines with catsup brought home from the hospital cafeteria.

I picked up another picture of Will with his father. It made me miss *my* father. He was the only one in my family that really understood my dancing dream. Every day after dance practice he'd let me demonstrate what I'd learned. Sometimes he'd even invite friends over and I'd have my own recital. I loved being the star of my own one woman show. But as I got older, I realized something wasn't right. Why was my father always home ready to watch my one woman show, while my mother worked two or three jobs in order to make ends meet? Apparently, my mother wondered the same thing.

"Did you buy the groceries?" she asked him one night when I was about twelve. She put her purse down and opened the refrigerator. It was empty.

"Baby, I had to use that money to pay back Curtis. I've been owein' him for a while. But don't worry, C.J. owes me $500. When he pays me, I'll pick up the groceries."

"My girls can't wait until C.J. decides to pay you back. What are they supposed to eat?" My mother tried to remain calm, but I could see she'd had enough.

"They're *our* girls and I'm sure you can find something in there to whip up for them. You're so good at that. You're like a miracle worker, Maxine." My father stood up and wrapped his arms around my mother as he kissed her neck. Usually, this melted my mother's anger and she'd forgive him once again. My father was a real charmer. His sweet words along with gorgeous movie star looks gave him such an advantage over her. He was so good looking that women often stuffed his pockets with their phone number even with my mother standing next to him.

"Get off me, Mario," she spat as she unwrapped herself from his arms. "I can't take this anymore. How many times are you gonna do this to us? That money was for food for the week. We have nothing." She placed her face in her hands and cried.

That night, my mother made us what she liked to call Jonny cakes. She would mix flour with water until it made a thick dough, then she'd pat them into these flat pancake type things. But without salt, baking powder or eggs, they were pretty disgusting. We ate them for a week.

Two weeks later, I came home from a dance class, bubbling with enthusiasm to show my father and Sasha this thing I learned called a frappe. It was the funniest little foot movement I had ever seen and I knew my father would think it was hilarious as well. But when I got home, he wasn't there. Sasha sat alone at the kitchen table.

"Daddy's gone," she said solemnly.

"Gone where?"

"I don't know," she said with a shrug. "And I don't care. Mommy kicked him out. It's about damn time too if you ask me."

"What?" I asked just as shocked by the fact that my mother actually stood up to my father as by the fact that my sister said 'damn'.

"He ruined us! Look at this place. Look at where we live because of him."

"It's not his fault. He just...he hasn't gotten his lucky break yet." I said optimistically as I set my dance bag on the floor and sat across from her. Sasha rested her head on her fist and looked off into space.

"Don't you miss our house?"

"Yeah, I do. But we'll be back there one day. Mommy promised."

"Get real. You need to accept that Mommy will never be able to get us out of this place. It's up to us. And once I'm out, I will never let a man drag me down like Daddy did to Mommy. I will never be with a poor man."

"Sasha, you can't decide who you fall in love with."

"Maybe not, but you sure can choose who you marry and I'm only marrying someone rich. I will never be poor again, no matter what."

I wasn't of the same opinion as Sasha, but I understood her. It did seem that my mother was so weak and in love that she allowed my father to ruin our lives. But I didn't think Sasha needed to go as far as marrying just for money. I began to wonder if that was the reason she dated Desmond.

A slamming door yanked me out of my memories. It was so loud I almost fell off the couch. I turned to see a red faced Will storm into the living room.

"Get back here, Will. I'm not finished." Julia yelled.

"I'm finished with you!" he roared back at her. Then as calmly as possible he grabbed my hand and said, "We're leaving."

"You're seriously gonna do this? What would our parents say?" Julia followed Will into the living room determined to keep the argument going as if I wasn't there.

"Don't you dare bring mom and dad into this!" The fierce, powerful tone of Will's voice made me shiver. Even Julia took a step back. He was so angry. "You have no right to even refer to them. You hadn't spoken to them for five years when they died. You have no idea what they were like or what they would want."

"I'm sure they wouldn't want you - ," Julia stopped mid-sentence and looked at me.

"What, Julia, what? Go ahead and say it right in front of her. Why don't you repeat those names you used earlier, huh?" Julia covered her mouth, then dashed into the kitchen. "I'm sure mom and dad wouldn't want you drinking yourself into a coma every night. Why don't you worry about your problems and let me live my own life!" Will pulled me out of the house.

I didn't realize I was crying until Will was speeding down the interstate. My face was hot and my heart ached. Will pulled into a rest stop. After putting the car in park, he brushed the tears away from my cheeks as he said, "Don't cry, Angel. Julia's an idiot. She has no idea what she's talking about."

"But I don't understand. She...she doesn't even know me," I whimpered.

"Exactly. She doesn't know you. If she knew you, she'd be just as crazy about you as I am; my parents, too."

"Really?" I asked, trying to gain some composure.

"Yeah, especially my mom. You two are so much alike." Will folded me into his arms. "I used to love the way she'd close her eyes when she played piano blocking out the rest of the world just like you do when you dance. You feel the music in a unique way just like she did. I miss her so much." Will held me as I rested my head on his chest and let his voice lull me to a state of peace and calm. "Even if you weren't incredibly talented and incredibly beautiful, they'd still love you. Once they saw how happy you make me, they would immediately welcome you into the family."

Even though I started to feel better about what happened with his sister, I still couldn't get it out of my mind.

"What's it like to be white?" I asked, interrupting him as he was telling me more about his parents.

"What do you mean?"

"I mean, are you constantly reminded that you're white or does it not even cross your mind?"

"I don't know. I never really thought about it."

"You see, I don't have that option. No matter what I do, I can't help but remember that I'm black."

"Is that a bad thing?"

"I don't know. It's just sometimes I feel like I don't know who or what I am. Even when I'm in...," I almost slipped and told him that I lived in Venton Heights, but thankfully, I caught myself and said, "...well...when I was in public school I was an outcast because I didn't like rap music or because I didn't know the latest slang. They made me feel like I wasn't black enough or something. And at Bridgeton, I can't help but stick out because I'm one of only a handful of black students there. Even as a ballerina, I don't think I'll ever be really accepted. Do you know someone actually wrote a letter to the newspaper complaining that I played Clara in The Nutcracker? It's like I'll never be white, but I'll also never be black enough to be black. I don't belong anywhere."

"I already told you. You belong with me." Will kissed the side of my head and squeezed me tightly.

We spent the rest of the evening in that rest area talking. Julia was still at home so we couldn't go there, the studio was having the floors refinished, and I still wasn't ready to take him to Venton Heights. So, we had nowhere else to go.

Chapter 17:
The Proposal

Friday morning, as soon as Will and I entered the main building of Bridgeton, there was a pronounced tension in the air. Students whispered and pointed down the hall. Even the teachers stood outside of their rooms trying to see what was happening. Will left my side for a second to ask one of his friends what was going on. Just then, I saw Colbert being escorted out of the building by two police officers. She was handcuffed! When she saw me she said, "Tell Sasha to watch her back."

What did that mean? Had Colbert been set up by the Bitch Brigade? Was Sasha next? A sense of dread ate away at my insides all day. I found Sasha and told her my fears, but she simply said, "Don't worry about it." Then she slammed her locker shut and stormed away. Something was bothering her.

Will knew I was upset and tried to make me feel better, by stuffing my locker full of white flowers and giving me a handmade card inviting me to dinner at his house that night. It didn't make me feel better, though. In fact, I felt even more nervous for some reason. Will was up to something. And it was big.

***

Will pulled out all the stops for dinner at his house that night. He decorated his living room and dining room with candles and played opera music in the background. He prepared bread with olive oil, lasagna, and even cannoli for dessert. It was incredibly romantic. A little too romantic, actually. I was afraid I'd missed some sort of special date for us. Were we celebrating something that I forgot?

"I have a confession to make," Will said while we were eating dessert. My heart raced. Did he cheat on me and make this fancy dinner to apologize? Maybe he was about to confess that he originally did want to use me for his Cherry Picker game? I shook the thought from my mind. I was totally overreacting. "I didn't actually make all this food," he said finally. "It came from the restaurant up the street," he added with a grin. I let out a sigh of relief.

"But there is a definite theme to the evening. Have you picked up on it yet?" he asked, smiling brightly like a child on Christmas.

I looked around and shrugged my shoulders. I didn't know what he was talking about.

"Well, the opera music, the food, the center piece in the shape of the leaning tower of Pisa."

"Italy?" I offered still not understanding what that had to do with anything.

"Yeah, Italy! I'm going to Italy next year. I just accepted a contract with a team in Rome. We can be together next year." Will rattled on excitedly about how we could get an apartment together in the city and have dinner together every night and make weekend trips to different European cities. He said he had never been to Europe and he looked forward to me showing him the parts I knew. I just sat there with a fake grin plastered on my face. I couldn't believe he had done this. I felt the walls of my life closing in on me. My world got smaller and smaller. I liked Will, I liked him a lot. But I didn't know if I could live with him.

"Will, I haven't been accepted to DiRisio, yet. I haven't even auditioned."

"It's just a matter of time, Babe. You'll make it. I know you will. They'll be crazy not to accept you."

"So you want us to live together in Rome?" I asked still a little stunned. I mean I hadn't even begun to think about what we would do next year. I didn't want to break up with him, but I hadn't even considered living together. I just thought we'd have a long distance relationship or something.

"I want us to do more than just live together," he said, standing and walking over to my side of the table. Then he pulled out a little black box, got down on one knee and said, "Marry me, Sonya."

"Marry you?" He nodded. My heartbeat accelerated, but it wasn't from excitement. I was scared to death. "Will, I'm only sixteen."

"You'll be seventeen in May."

"That's not the point."

"I know. I know. The point is, I want to spend the rest of my life with you. I'm not saying we have to do it today or tomorrow, maybe not even next year. I just want you to wear this ring and know that you're mine."

"Know that I'm yours? Like you own me?"

"You know that's not what I meant." He took the ring out of the box and slipped it onto my limp finger. "It was my mother's engagement ring. It looks beautiful on you."

I couldn't breathe. I seriously thought I was going to hyperventilate. This was too much pressure. I couldn't do this. I couldn't promise myself to him and wear his dead mother's ring. I was only sixteen. We'd only known each other for a few weeks and before that he was a sex addict.

"I can't do this, Will."

"What?" He stared at me with eyes that suddenly looked sad again. He looked truly hurt by my reaction, but I had to tell him how I really felt. "But, last week in the gym, you said you wanted me to be your one and only. I thought that meant -"

"I know what I said, Will. I know. I just...I can't..." I placed my head in my hands and tried to collect my thoughts. "Will, you're a great person and I love talking to you and being with you, but...I feel like...I can't breathe...I feel like you've made me your everything. I can't...it's too much...you're suffocating me. I need some space."

Will sighed, swallowed hard and said, "Okay." He slipped the ring off my finger and placed it back in the little black box. Then he stood up and walked to his side of the table, the whole time not making eye contact with me.

"Okay? That's it?"

"You don't want to marry me. What else do you want me to say?"

"Tell me you understand why. Tell me you're not mad at me."

"I understand and I'm not mad at you." His voice was short and clipped as if holding back what he really felt or wanted to say. He was shutting down emotionally. I felt like I was killing him.

He sat back in his seat and stared at his perfectly sectioned food.

"Will, talk to me."

He closed his eyes and shook his head. "Not now."

"Will, I'm not saying I want to break up with you I just can't agree to marry you. Not so soon."

He nodded. "I said, I understand."

I'm not sure if he did.

Moments later I sat at a bus stop crying my eyes out and rubbing the spot where Will's mother's ring once sat. I felt like the scum of the earth. No, I felt worse than scum. I felt like what scum poops out. How could I not want to marry him? Was I crazy? Wouldn't every girl in the world jump at the chance to have a guy like Will forever? But then again, maybe I wasn't the crazy one. Who in the world proposes to their sixteen year old girlfriend after only dating her for like two months? It seemed like Will was using me as the cure-all for his personal problems. I couldn't take that kind of pressure.

I was supposed to go to the studio for a class, but I couldn't bring myself to do it. I would've spent the entire time thinking about Will. Ms. Alexander would've just yelled at me for not being focused. Sasha was out with Des, my mother was working. Sitting at home alone was out of the question. I didn't know where to go or what to do.

That's when I noticed a blue Audi with tinted windows pass by me for the second, maybe third time. Then it pulled right in front of the bus stop and the dark window slowly slid down. I turned away. "Are you alright?" a deep voice said.

"Fine. I'm just fine." I sniffled. The last thing I needed was for some loser to try to pick me up on the side of the street. Obviously, the man in the car didn't pick up on my dismissive tone because the car engine stopped and I heard the door open. I grabbed hold of my belongings tightly. What if he was going to mug me? Just as I was about to hop off the bench and make a run for it, I got a glimpse of David's perfect green eyes. "You're obviously not fine." He handed me a handkerchief and sat next to me. "Want to talk about it?" I shook my head, wiping my tears. "Well, I hate to see a beautiful woman cry. How about you let me try to cheer you up?" I shrugged. It was better than being alone.

***

David's house was almost an exact replica of Will's, big, white and fancy. It was about three blocks away in the same ritzy neighborhood where every yard was perfectly manicured and even the mailboxes looked expensive.

"I'm so happy I'm going to get to spend some time with you," David said, taking my coat and bag and placing them in the closet by the front door. "I've had my eye on you for a while." He winked at me and flashed that dashing smile that I'd coveted for over a year.

"Really?" My eyes expanded in excitement. I knew I shouldn't have been so affected by his attention but this was David Winthrop! I'd been completely in love with him for almost my entire time at Bridgeton. Old habits are very hard to break.

"Yeah. I've always thought you were cute. When Maddox swept you up I thought I'd lost my chance. But I get the feeling there's trouble in paradise."

David reached out and caressed my cheek. I had to turn away. There was no way I could look into David's eyes while thinking about Will. I'd probably hurt Will so much tonight. Just being in David's house felt like cheating. But maybe this is what Will and I needed. I couldn't promise myself to my first boyfriend. I kinda needed to see what else was out there.

David must have picked up on my anxiety. "Hey, wait a minute. I said I was going to cheer you up. Wait here," he said, jogging into another room.

Suddenly I heard music. It was the intro to "The Way You Look Tonight." Then David came up behind me, grabbed my hand, swung me around and landed me in a dip.

"Someday, when I'm awfully low," he serenaded while turning me around and around the foyer under the circular staircase. An elegant chandelier hung above our heads and for a moment, I felt giddy. I closed my eyes and was swept away by the music and David's strong dancing lead. *"When the world is cold, I will feel a glow just thinking of you. And the way you look tonight."* David's attempt to make me feel better did that and more. Combining dance and David's sumptuous singing voice was nothing short of magic. But then an image of Will popped into my head. Weird, creepy, intense, yet sweet and fragile Will. Will may have had his faults but he didn't deserve this kind of treatment. He didn't deserve me cheating on him.

Just when I was about to push away from David, I felt his lips on my face. I can't really say they were on my lips because they were actually on my face. They were wet and messy and everywhere. I had to hold in a laugh at how bad a kisser he was. I couldn't believe I used to dream about this moment. Will was such a better kisser. I missed Will.

"What? What's the problem?" David asked when I pulled away.

"I just had a rough night. I'm not really in the mood."

"Really?" He sounded shocked. I was kinda shocked myself. I mean, I'd had a crush on David Winthrop for over a year and now I had him and I felt nothing.

David's face changed. I thought a saw a hint of anger

in his eyes. He was obviously not used to rejection. Just when he was about to say something, the doorbell rang.

While he went to answer the door, I decided it was time to leave. But that wasn't going to be easy.

"Hey, David. Is she still here?" I heard someone say. I instantly recognized the sickly sweet voice of Ashley Carter.

Oh, it was definitely time to go. I opened the front closet and grabbed my coat and bag, just as Ashley, followed by Lauren and another girl stepped through the front door.

"Are you leaving already, Sonya?" Lauren asked.

I just rolled my eyes and tried to get past them to the door, but they wouldn't let me through.

"Look, Sonya, before you go I just want to…apologize to you," Ashley said.

"Apologize?" I was slightly confused. Ashley didn't really seem like the apologizing type.

"Yeah, I'm really sorry about showing you the Cherry Picker thing. That was really bitchy of me."

"Uh-huh," I said still skeptical that this was genuine.

"I guess I was just jealous. But I'm happy for you now. I mean, Will must really love you. He told Poe that he wanted to marry you."

"Poe? Who's Poe?"

"He's my boyfriend," Lauren volunteered. "His real

name's Edgar Allen. He's captain of the basketball team."

"Oh, I get it. Edgar Allen Poe. Right. Got it." How in the world could I date a basketball player for two months and not know the captain of the team? I was so oblivious sometimes.

"So, are you going to marry him?" Ashley asked.

My heartbeat accelerated again. Not only had Will proposed to me after only a few weeks of dating, he had also told his friends. What was he thinking? He was serious about this. Really serious. What if my rejection sent him over the edge? What if he attempted suicide again because of me? This was too much. I couldn't breathe again.

"Are you okay?' David asked.

"I...I think...I'm hyperventilating."

Lauren and Ashley led me to the living room and sat me down on the couch.

"Brittany, get her something to drink," Lauren said, sitting down next to me.

Seconds later, a girl with strawberry blonde hair handed me a glass of lemonade. I recognized her from the school play a few months back where she played opposite David. I wished I could have complimented her on it, but she was actually pretty bad. I remember thinking it was a horrible casting decision.

"Was it something we said? We didn't mean to upset you," Lauren said, rubbing my back.

"It's not...your fault, Lauren. I just -"

"DeHaven." She interrupted me.

"What?"

"My name is Lauren *DeHaven*."

I just stared at her completely confused. What the hell was the difference? Once again, I got that creepy vibe from Lauren. Something just wasn't right about that girl.

After focusing on my breathing for a few minutes, I decided it was time to leave. I needed to get to Will. I needed to let him know that I did care about him even though I wasn't ready to marry him. I needed to make sure he was okay.

"I better go now," I said, chugging the last of the lemonade. I stood up, but then got so dizzy I had to sit back down.

"Why don't you relax for a little bit? You're upset. You're in no condition to go home alone," Brittany said.

"Don't worry, we'll take good care of you." Ashley added with her sweet yet creepy smile.

***

The next thing I remember I lay on a gloriously cold bathroom floor. It felt so good to be cold I actually rubbed my face against the tile. Then someone knelt over me, lifted my head and wiped my face with a cool rag. It was Sasha.

"What are you doing here?" I asked. I tried to get up,

but the room started spinning.

"Don't get up," she said in her 'you're in trouble' tone. The last time she sounded like that was when she found out I failed a Chemistry quiz.

"What's wrong with my head?" I asked as I felt my scalp to make sure there wasn't a knife sticking out of it.

"You've got a hangover. What were you thinking? You've never had a drink in your life. What made you think you could handle all that alcohol?"

"What are you talking about? I didn't drink anything."

"Then how do you explain this?" Sasha showed me a picture on her camera phone. It was me in my underwear dancing on a table.

Chapter 18:
The Bitch Brigade Strikes

"Where did you get that?" I exclaimed horrified at what I had unwittingly done.

"Around 10:00 last night someone sent this to me. Desi and I immediately went to David's house and got you out of there before you did anything else I knew you'd regret." Sasha slammed her phone shut and yelled, "What were you thinking?"

"I don't know what happened? I don't remember getting drunk. All I had was lemonade."

"That wasn't lemonade!" she yelled, standing. Her voice echoed causing every fiber in my body to twitch. She had no idea how much pain just the sound of her voice caused. If she did, she would surely lower it. I tried to cover my ears and block out some of the sound as she said, "It's called grain alcohol. It's odorless, colorless, and 80 proof." I didn't know what 80 proof meant, but I felt like now wasn't the time to ask. I probably should've learned it in Chemistry class. I immediately recalled Will's advice to never drink anything that wasn't in a factory-sealed container. Why didn't I think of that last night?

Sasha paced the bathroom. When did our bathroom get big enough for pacing? The last time I checked our bathroom was barely big enough to hold me and Sasha at the same time. I looked around. This wasn't our bathroom.

"Where are we?"

"We're at Desi's house. I couldn't have him take us home and you were in no condition to walk. So we spent the night here." She crossed her arms and continued pacing. "How are we going to fix this?" she asked more to herself than to me.

"I'll just explain to everyone that I didn't know I was drinking and that it really wasn't like me and…" Sasha stopped in her tracks, spun around and glared at me causing me to freeze mid-sentence.

"Do you have absolutely no idea how high school works? No one cares you didn't know you were drunk. This is going to haunt you for the rest of your time at Bridgeton. It's going to haunt *us*! I bet most of the people there thought you were me!" Just then, I heard a knock on the bathroom door.

"What!" Sasha barked at the intruder. I had never seen her so angry before about anything.

An always polite Desmond asked if we were coming down for breakfast. Sasha softened a little. "Maybe later, Babe," she said, trying to sound sweet for Desmond's sake. The thought of food made my stomach turn. I pulled myself up on one arm and leaned over the toilet just as everything I ever ate in my life spewed out of my mouth. Sasha came to my side, held my hair and rubbed my back.

"I'm so sorry, Sweetie. I'm so sorry you had to learn the hard way not to trust the Bitch Brigade," she said as she wiped my mouth with the cloth.

"I'm sorry," I moaned. I closed my eyes and tried to remember when things went wrong. I remembered talking to the bitches. And I did trust them momentarily. I believed their apology and I took the drink from them. And then I was dancing and doing a whole bunch of other stuff with... "Oh God, David," I said in panic.

"Yes David. Why don't we talk about David? Didn't I tell you he was an asshole? Didn't I tell you not to trust him? What were you thinking? I tell you what you should've been thinking."

"Did I...you know...do anything with David?" I said between sobs.

"Nothing too serious. Just a lap dance according to the pictures."

"Just a lap dance? Just a lap dance! Oh God, Will is going to hate me. He's never going to talk to me again. Wait, does he know?"

"Sweetie, everyone with a cell phone, email, or a

pulse knows, but..." I started bawling again. "Shhh, I'm not done. He was here at 5:30 this morning looking for you. He's worried about you. I told him to come back later."

"No, I can't face him. I can't." Surely, he wanted to see me in order to break up with me. I wanted more space and I bet now he was willing to give me all the space I wanted, permanently.

Sasha tucked me into bed as I cried myself to sleep. I actually dreamt that last night didn't happen and that Will still loved me, but then I woke up and saw that I was still in Des' house. Reality pounded me in the head. Or that could have been the hangover. I turned and looked at the clock: 1:27 in the afternoon.

"Will is downstairs," Sasha said through the door after a quick knock. "Get yourself together and come talk to him."

"I can't," I whined on the verge of tears again.

"That wasn't a request," she said curtly. Something in her tone made me hop out of bed without another thought of protest.

On my way down the stairs, I heard Sasha and Will in the den.

"She's on her way. You better hope I can fix this or I'm coming after you," she said to him.

"Me? What did I do?"

"Oh, please. You know this is all your fault, right?"

"*My* fault? What the hell are you talking about?"

"She should've broken up with you when I told her to."

"You told her to break up with me? How could you? I love her."

"Love?" Sasha laughed a little. "Please. You're a psycho. A freaking psycho. First you stalk her for two months while screwing every girl in sight, then now suddenly you're in love. Is this some sort of game to you? I swear to God if you hurt her I will ruin your life."

Will clapped his hands dramatically.

"Stellar performance, Sasha, really. Is there a camera nearby?"

"Shut up!"

"Come off it, Sasha. You may have everyone else fooled but not me. *Your* friends did this. I bet you're only angry that you didn't think of it first."

Sasha slapped him. "Go to hell!" she yelled before storming off.

Will stood in the den rubbing his still red cheek and staring out of the window. I hesitated a moment at the entrance and just looked at him. He was so handsome. The sun shined on his hair making shades of gold dance on every strand. I hated myself for hurting him so much.

I wanted to ask about the conversation I'd just

overheard. It seemed as though Will thought he know something about my sister that I didn't. How could he call those girls friends of Sasha? Didn't he know how afraid of them she was?

Now wasn't the time to talk about Sasha, though. Will and I had a lot of things to work out in our relationship.

"Do you hate me?" I asked.

"I could never hate you," he said still staring out of the window.

"Are you angry with me?"

He shrugged. "I'm not angry. I'm just...I just don't understand. I poured my heart out to you. I asked you to be my wife and then you run right into David's arms."

"But Will, that's part of the problem. You asked me to marry you. I'm sixteen and I've only known you for what? Three months tops? How could you possibly expect me to marry you?"

"You want David, don't you? You're never going to feel for me what I feel for you," he said as if he didn't hear me.

"Will, you're not listening. David is not the issue here. That's the one thing I've figured out. You're what I want, but we need to get to know each other better. We need to slow it down a little, okay?"

He didn't answer me. We fell into a tense silence as Will kept staring out the window. I felt like I might have lost him forever.

"Do you want to break up?" I asked finally.

He shook his head and asked, "Do you want to break up with me?"

"No, but I can't marry you, Will. Not now."

He sighed. "I know. It was stupid of me to try to force that on you. It's just that...I lost everyone and everything I ever loved. And then you came along and make me feel..." He leaned his head against the glass and said, "I guess I just tried to hold on to you too tight. I'm sorry."

"Don't apologize. We both made mistakes last night."

Will crossed the room and embraced me. "Your only mistake was being too trusting. You were tricked."

"What am I gonna do? Sasha says those girls are gonna make my life miserable," I said burying my head into his chest and drinking in his scent. I felt so safe in his arms. Too bad I wasn't safe, not from the Bitch Brigade.

"She would know," he said sitting down on the couch with me still in his arms.

"What does *that* mean? Why were you two fighting just now?"

He kissed the top of my head. "We both care about you a lot and we're just…upset this happened. There's no telling what they'll do next."

My thoughts went back to the girl in the stairwell.

What if they did the same thing to me? "Is there any chance they'll just forget about me and move on?"

"No, there's no chance of that. I already told you," Sasha said, marching into the den with her laptop in tow. "They're going to make your life a living hell. Look at this. They've already made a website and a facebook page with all the pictures from last night." Sasha set the laptop on the coffee table and started scrolling down the pictures. There had to be at least 20 of them each increasingly more vulgar. Apparently, I had been doing some sort of striptease. I couldn't look anymore. I turned away and buried my face in Will's chest again.

"And don't even get me started on the YouTube video." Sasha closed her eyes and shook her head for a second. "This is even worse than what they did to Leila Baker last year."

"What'd they do to her?" I asked. Sasha glared at me again.

"They started this ridiculous rumor that she was having an affair with her father," Will volunteered.

"Oh my God, that's awful," I said horrified at the thought.

"It got to the point where she couldn't walk down the halls without people calling her 'Daddy's girl'. She ended up leaving Bridgeton 'cause she couldn't take it anymore," he added.

"But why would anyone even believe that?" I asked.

"Because those bitches are evil geniuses," Sasha said. "They knew Leila came from a close knit family. You know, one of those families who kiss on the lips. They took that and ran with it."

"Why is this worse?"

"Because this time they have pictures and video!" Sasha roared as if I was the biggest idiot in the world for not understanding that. Will squeezed me tighter.

"There's no need to yell at her. She feels bad enough," Will said. Sasha glared at him.

"Why do they have so much power? Why does everyone believe what they say and just do what they want?" I asked.

"Because they're pretty, popular, and rich. They have what everyone wants. And they usually get whatever they want. But you got in their way. You took what they thought was rightfully theirs; the star basketball player." Sasha gestured to Will.

"I can't believe I was ever with Ashley. What was I thinking?"

"You were thinking with the wrong head. Next time why don't you keep it zipped up, huh?"

"You need to get off your God damn high horse, Sasha, before I -"

"Sasha, Will, please stop fighting. You're making me feel even worse. This is my fault for falling for such a childish trap. I should've been more careful."

Sasha and Will glared at each other both seething with anger. Finally, Sasha broke the tension and turned away.

"So, I've been working this out in my head all day," Sasha said after pacing the length of the den several times. She moved away from a sarcastic bitter tone to her all business tone. "I think we have three options in how to deal with this. Option number 1, you switch schools. That's out of the question, because your only choice is to go back to public school. I'm not gonna let that happen. Option number 2, we get Des' father to sue the Bitch Brigade for defamation of character or criminal negligence or something. The problem with this is that it paints you as a victim and doesn't work toward restoration of your damaged character."

"Bitch Brigade?" Will asked when Sasha stopped for a breath. "You mean that's real?"

"That's what I said." Well at least I wasn't the only one who thought the Bitch Brigade was an urban legend.

"So that leads me to option 3," she continued ignoring our interruption. "We face it head-on."

"What do you mean face it head-on?" I asked.

"We embrace this image they're trying to give to you. If we make it seem like you did this on purpose, there is no joy they can extract from taunting you with it. We make it seem like *their* taunts are part of *your* plan."

"What plan? My plan to look like a slut? Sasha, I don't see how this is gonna work."

"No, hear me out," she said, getting excited. Her brain worked faster than she could talk. "What they want is to destroy you, to humiliate you. If you turn everything they do around and do it better they'll have nothing to stand on."

"Like what?"

"Like, I bet right now they're at Kinko's printing up flyers with you in your underwear to pass out at school. We could print up flyers too and pass them out. I can go online and start a rumor that you were a lingerie model in Europe and that's why you're so comfortable in your underwear. We can show some of the publicity shots you took in Barcelona. You have one in a pretty skimpy costume right? Do you see where I'm going with this?"

"I think so," I said unable to hide my skepticism. I looked over at Will and he seemed a bit more convinced.

"This could work," he said.

"But why the flyers? Why would I pass out pictures of myself like that?"

"They could be campaign flyers," Will volunteered.

"Good idea. Finally, a worthwhile contribution from you," Sasha said to Will with a sneer.

"Campaign flyers? Campaign flyers for what?" I asked. Sasha and Will were at a loss.

Then out of nowhere Desmond said, "Prom Queen."

"Oh my God, honey, you're brilliant!" Sasha exclaimed as she rewarded him with a kiss. Then she turned to me and said, "You're going to be Bridgeton's next queen if it's the last thing I do."

Chapter 19:
Rumors

"But I don't want to be Prom Queen," I said terrified at the prospect. The Prom queen had to give a speech; in front of people. Because, of course, a speech would have to be in front of people. I didn't do speeches. Now, I could get in front of a group f people and dance. I could even get in front of a group of people and *talk* about dance. But any other subject and I panicked in front of a crowd. I couldn't help but think back to the bathroom conversation incident.

"I really don't care what you want to be," Sasha snapped at me again. It shocked me how quickly she went from excited to angry. "This is just to divert people's attention off of the fact that you got plastered at a party and stripped. If you can't get through this you might as well transfer or…kill yourself."

I felt Will tense up. How could she say something like that? She had no idea how she was hurting both of us. Will looked away, not wanting Sasha to even be in his line of sight anymore. "She didn't mean anything by that," I whispered to Will.

Sasha knelt in front of the laptop and started typing furiously for a few minutes. "Now there are a couple of key elements we have to make sure are addressed," she said looking up from the screen. "Number 1: we have to make sure everyone knows we are two different people. So, I will be your campaign manager," Sasha stood and paced the room again. "Number 2: this whole episode occurred because of your relationship with Will, so we have to show everyone that you two are stronger than ever. If they see they've failed to drive you apart, they may give up. So, Will, you have to support her like crazy. I want to see public displays of affection everywhere." Sasha knelt in front of the laptop again and typed. She checked all the social websites that Bridgeton students frequented trying to find the next party and she started sending anonymous emails to the popular kids. Will, Desmond, and I just watched her operate, all afraid to interrupt her thought process. "Okay, the plan starts tonight," she continued. "There's a party at Caitlin Tuten-Rhodes' house and we're all going."

Sasha spent the rest of the day planting rumors about my non-existent modeling career and convincing me I needed a sexy outfit for the party that night. I was completely mortified. She actually wanted me to do another impromptu striptease. She also coached me on what to say to the Bitch Brigade if they had any comments for me.

"Brittany is the ugly one," Sasha explained while she

straightened my hair with a flat iron. "The liposuction, the nose job, and the boob job have helped, but there is just no hope for her smile. The girl looks like Mr. Ed. If she says anything to you just say something like, 'hey, horse mouth, I think your chest is leaking'."

I thought about Brittany's appearance for a moment. She did look like a horse. Under normal circumstances, I would never result to childish petty insults, but I wasn't about to oppose Sasha so I just sighed and said, "Fine, what else."

"Now on to Ashley. Ashley is a whore. If Ashley says anything to you, just say that Will told you that her vajayjay smelled like fish or that she was so loose having sex with her was like throwing a hot dog down a hallway."

"Sasha, I can't say those things! It's just not like me." I turned around in the chair and looked at her. My eyes pleaded with her to try to think of another way. There had to be something else I could say that wasn't so crass. "I can barely believe those thoughts would even cross your mind. When did you start using that language? There has to be another way," I said.

"Fine, then say that Will got tired of having to wait in line every time he wanted to stick it in."

"No, I will not! Besides, Will didn't say those things."

"Well, ask him about it. I'm sure he'll agree with me," she said as she turned me around and resumed her efforts with my hair.

"No, he won't. He's different now."

"That's what *you* think."

"What's that supposed to mean?"

"Nothing. Let's just move on to Lauren DeHaven. She's the biggest bitch of them all. Do you know what she did to Naseem, the exchange student from Iran?" she asked kind of rhetorically since she didn't give me a chance to respond. "Her first day at school Lauren DeHaven told her that the word for 'meet' was actually another four letter word that begins with 'F'. The poor girl went up to everyone that day saying 'pleased to F you'. I still can't believe you took a drink from her." Sasha shook her head disapprovingly. "But I have so much dirt on her, she is going to rue the day she crossed us. First of all, her father is about to declare bankruptcy. He made some awful investments and her family is practically broke. Her mother left her father and ran off with their accountant and her brother is so addicted to pain killers he's been in rehab twice in the past year."

"Sasha, how do you know all this?"

"Don't worry about it. Now, even though she's dating Poe, I know for a fact she's a lesbian or at least bi."

I sighed and shook my head. This was too much for me to handle. "Sasha, I don't want to have to spread rumors about people."

"It's not a rumor if it's true. And this is definitely true. In fact, I have video."

"What!"

"You heard me. I. Have. Video," she said

emphasizing each word. "If she says anything at all to you just say three words: Lauren, Brooke, video. Then walk away. She will be so shocked she'll probably wet herself. Leaving the DeHaven off of her name will be like an added kick in the stomach. She hates that. She refuses to be confused with Lauren Holloway, Lauren Rovick, Lauren Smith or Lauren Widman."

I couldn't believe my sister's words. I couldn't believe my sister was privy to this kind of information. How utterly scandalous and crude.

"Sasha, seriously, why do you know all this stuff? *How* do you know this?"

"I said, don't worry about it," she said curtly.

But I couldn't help worrying about it. There had to be a reason Sasha knew all of this. I thought back to what I overheard Will say earlier. Was it possible that Sasha was friends with these girls? I needed to know the truth.

"Sasha," I said changing the tone of our rumor fest. "I overheard you and Will arguing today."

She put down the flat iron and crossed her arms. She took a deep breath and said, "I'm sorry you had to hear that. I'm sorry I don't like your boyfriend."

I shook my head. "No, that's not what I'm concerned about. I know you don't like Will for me. I'm worried about something he said."

Sasha raised her eyebrow waiting for me to continue.

"He said they were your friends." She didn't respond. "Are they really your friends, Sasha? Did you know anything about what they did to me?"

Sasha's bottom lip started quivering. "How could you even ask me that?" she said as a tear spilled down her face. She turned away from me. Suddenly I felt guilty for even thinking it.

"Two years ago, during my first week of school," Sasha began in a hushed voice, "they tried to befriend me." She turned and leaned against the sink. "I thought they really liked me. I thought I found a place to belong."

She stopped abruptly.

"What happened?" I asked.

Sasha closed her eyes tightly as if holding back more tears. Then in one swift movement, she whipped off her hair. I gasped.

"You're wearing a wig?" I stood up and studied her hair or what was left of it. There were bald spots in between short unhealthy patches of hair.

She nodded while letting the tears flow. "They got close enough to me to fill my shampoo bottle with Nair. When I tried to wash my hair after gym class, it came out in clumps. It hasn't grown back properly since."

"Oh, Sasha," I said hugging her and letting her cry on my shoulder. I wanted to ask her why she couldn't smell the Nair before she used it. I mean that's pretty strong stuff. But I didn't want to make her feel any worse.

"I…never…told anyone," she said between short shallow breaths as she tried to control her sobbing. "I just bought a wig and pretended it never happened. I've stayed away from them since."

"Oh, Sasha, I'm so sorry."

"Don't be." Sasha took a deep breath. She placed her wig back on her head and then wiped away the last of her tears. "I got over it. I didn't let them get to me and I rose to student body president. You can get through this too. You just have to trust me." She sat me back down in the chair and stared into my eyes. "I know you think this is beneath you and petty, but really this is the only way to defeat them. I can fix this, but you have to trust me, sweetie, okay?"

"Okay," I said reluctantly.

Sasha hugged me and started working on my make-up.

"Good, I'm glad we're in agreement on this. Now," she said changing her mood. She went from sad back to vindictive in the blink of an eye, "Lauren DeHaven is going to be your greatest opponent for prom queen since Poe is a shoe in for King. So really watch your back for her."

***

I had to admit, when she was done I looked like a supermodel. I could have been on the cover of any one of those fashion magazines I always passed up for dance magazines. The tiny skirt Sasha made me wear really accentuated my long shapely dancer legs. And the top was just short enough to reveal a hint of my rock solid abdomen.

Even Will was shocked by my transformation.

"I mean, not to say you weren't beautiful before," he said after stumbling over his words for a few minutes. "I think you're gorgeous either way, but I can definitely deal with this for a night or two."

When we got to the party, my nervous stomach almost made me puke again. Sasha told me to just pretend like I played a character in a famous ballet. She said that if her plan worked, no one would even remember or care by the next weekend and then I could go back to normal.

Will and I burst into the party like we owned the place. We danced in the middle of the floor and groped each other for most of the night. Out of the corner of my eye I could see Ashley fuming. Then, when the right song came on, I took center stage, or center living room, and did my thing. Everyone chanted my name again, but this time, I had planned it. I even incorporated some ballet moves into my act and get some oh's and ah's when I went into my splits.

By the end of the night, I was the life of the party. The underwear model rumor had taken flight and a few guys asked to take a picture with me.

At some point, Will and I got separated. He went off to talk with his buddies as I made rounds trying to show how supremely confident with my body I was. Then, suddenly, someone pulled me into a bedroom. Lips kissed me and hands touched me all over. I could immediately tell it wasn't Will. I pushed him off and got a good look at an inebriated David Winthrop. I didn't remember how far I had gone with him the night before, but apparently it was far enough for him to think he had an open invitation to my body.

"Get off me!" I yelled as I tried to fight him.

"You know you want me," he slurred. In that moment, I couldn't think of one reason why I had been so infatuated with him. What was I thinking?

"Maybe I wanted you in the past, but I have a boyfriend now," I said, stepping away from him and preparing to bolt out the door if he tried anything.

"So, that's it?" He seemed a little disappointed. I wondered for a moment if he actually liked me. Then I couldn't help but wonder if he was just drunk and horny or if he just thought I was Sasha again.

"I thought we made a connection last night," David said, sitting on the bed. I almost went and sat next to him. I got a quick flash of all those fantasies I used to have of him. It would've been so easy to make one of them come true right there and then. But something kept me from going over to him on the bed. Something didn't feel right. I didn't know whether I had suddenly become paranoid because of what happened the night before, but I felt the need to get out of that room, fast. So, that's what I did. I didn't even say another word to David, I just ran out as he babbled something about it not being a good idea that I reject him.

"Do you know what I can do to you?" I heard him say. Good thing I left when I did. Just as I walked out of the room, I saw Ashley dragging Will around the corner. That little witch was trying to set me up again. She wanted Will to catch me with David. How could someone be so evil? I ducked around the corner and watched with delight as her plan failed miserably.

"I swear I saw her come in here with him," she said after they had walked into the room. Will just shook her loose and charged out of the door. "Wait, Will, wait!" she called, scurrying after him.

When Ashley's attempt to turn Will against me failed, Brittany and Lauren DeHaven tried the intimidation approach. They forced me into an empty room and said, "You have no idea who you're playing with." Lauren DeHaven shoved my shoulder like she wanted to fight and I had to hold in a laugh. She was a good three inches shorter than me. I could have leveled her with one swift arabesque to her chest. She had no idea how many fights I had been in with much more formidable opponents in Venton Heights.

"I suggest you never touch me again," I said calmly.

"Oh, yeah, well what are you gonna do?"

"I have three words for you. Lauren, Brooke, video." I crossed my arms and glared at her. Lauren DeHaven's eyes expanded and her jaw dropped.

"How do you...where did you...," she stuttered.

"What is she talking about, LD?" Brittany asked. This must have been a piece of information even her closest friends didn't know about. I still wondered how Sasha knew.

"Sasha!" she gasped as she turned around and stormed out of the room leaving a confused Brittany behind.

"Do you have anything to add, horse face?"

Brittany's mouth flew open in shock. I kinda shocked myself at my own cruelty. Then she scampered off after Lauren DeHaven.

I was relieved when my 'show' ended and we could leave the party. I'd had enough of the high school party scene. Too bad it had taken the Bitch Brigade to make me realize it. Sasha was extremely pleased with how well her plan worked. By Monday, no one pitied me or ridiculed the girl who had been duped by the Bitch Brigade. Instead, guys were high-fiving Will in the hall and girls were asking me what it was like to work in Europe. I actually gave them detailed accounts of photo shoots since I had done several for the dance festival I attended in Spain. It wasn't the best image or reputation to have in high school, but it beat being portrayed as a weak pitiful victim who can't handle her alcohol. The only drawback: yeah, possibly winning prom queen.

Chapter 20:
This Ain't Over

Already convinced that I'd win prom queen, Sasha wanted me to look the part. Originally, she had planned for me to wear the black and pink cocktail dress she wore last year, but at the last minute she decided against it. She thought someone might remember it. So that morning, she bought me a white empire-waist gown with red detailing. It looked almost like a wedding dress. By the time she finished putting my hair in an up do with cascading tendrils, I really did look like a queen.

Des rented a limousine for the night and somehow Sasha convinced him it would be more time efficient if the limousine picked up Sasha and me, then Will, then Des. Of course, the limo never came to Venton Heights. Sasha and I met the driver at the rental place and left from there.

Sometime during dinner, the significance of what was about to happen registered in my mind. The student

population of Bridgeton had voted on whether they liked me
or not. Of course, I knew I shouldn't really care, but I did. I
wanted to be liked, which meant I wanted to win. But then
again, I didn't want to win. The winner had to go on stage
and give an acceptance speech. What if I said something
stupid? What if I didn't say anything at all?

By the time dessert came, I nervously tapped my
finger on the table. I made the silverware clink, causing
people in the fancy French restaurant to stare at me. Sasha
gave me a look that said 'relax' or possibly 'relax, you idiot',
but I couldn't stop. Will placed his hand over mine which
made my finger stop, but then my leg picked up where my
finger left off causing the whole table to shake from my knee
banging the bottom of it. I realized I was being ridiculous,
but the idea of me as prom queen was even more ridiculous.
If I won, I couldn't stand up in front of everyone and make a
speech. And if I didn't win, that would mean no one liked me.
Either way, I felt trapped. I felt trapped in this restaurant. I
couldn't breathe. No, I couldn't go through with this. What a
stupid idea. I had to tell Sasha her plan wasn't going to work.
I had to get out of this. I had to get out of there.

"Okay, let's go for a walk," Will said, standing up
from the table.

"So, tell me exactly why you're nervous," he said
once we were outside and walking around the block. "I have
seen you dance alone on stage in front of a sold out audience.
You weren't nervous then. What is it about giving a 20-
second speech that throws you into a panic?"

"Dancing is different. I'd give my firstborn child to be
able to dance instead of give that speech."

"Hey, don't go bartering off our children like that," Will teased.

"I'm serious, Will. This freaks me out. I hope I don't win. What am I gonna do if I win? What am I gonna say? I never know what to say to people. I wish you could be on stage with me. Why aren't you running for king?"

"I won last year, Babe. I can't run twice in a row."

"Duh! I knew that. You see how stupid I am? I'm too stupid to give a speech." I said, slipping into full panic mode. "Oh, I wish I were Sasha, she always says the right thing."

"Stop saying things like that," he said firmly as he stopped and stepped in front of me. "You're not stupid and you're not Sasha, thank God. You're *you* and *you* are the greatest person I've ever met in my life." Will wrapped me in his arms after planting a passionate kiss on my lips.

When the time to announce the king and queen came, all of the nominees went on stage. Lauren DeHaven hugged me and the other three girls running against her as if we were all part of this big happy family. She pretended like she'd be equally happy if either of us won. What a fake bitch, I thought.

Sasha, as student body president, opened the envelope for king first and, of course, it was Poe. Lauren DeHaven cheered for her boyfriend as he made his speech in which he mentioned the state champion basketball team. I wondered if I could somehow mention the basketball team in my speech if I won. But that wouldn't make any sense. As Sasha opened the envelope for queen, Lauren DeHaven actually grabbed my hand and the hand of the girl next to her.

When Sasha read my name off the card, Lauren DeHaven squeezed my hand so hard I thought she might snap my fingers off. Then she hugged me and whispered in my ear, "This ain't over."

Sasha jumped up and down in excitement as they placed the crown on my head. I was too shocked to jump up and down. I was too shocked to move. I felt completely stiff and frozen as Sasha hugged me and whispered, "Breathe, don't forget to breathe." But I forgot to breathe. I forgot everything. All I saw was that microphone looming in front of me. With each second it grew bigger and bigger. And it was mocking me. Logic told me it was impossible for an inanimate object to mock someone, but I swear that microphone had it in for me. It told me that in a matter of seconds everyone in the school would see what an idiot I was and they'd immediately strip me of my crown.

The audience drew quiet as they waited for me to take the microphone and say something profound.

Sasha hugged me again and inconspicuously pushed me toward the microphone, but then at the last second she grabbed it and said, "Ladies and Gentlemen, I know the queen is the one who is supposed to talk right now, but I really couldn't pass up the opportunity to tell everyone how incredibly proud I am of my beautiful and talented little sister. You did the right thing by choosing the sweetest, kindest, most deserving person at Bridgeton. She is the best sister anyone could have and the best queen Bridgeton could have."

I appreciated Sasha standing up for me and saving me once again, but somehow I felt I needed to stand on my own for once. I was no longer a loser who ran into cows, waited patiently while the popular kids blocked her locker, or babbled about public urination. I was a queen and I needed to act like one. I tapped Sasha on the shoulder and gestured for the mic. Her eyes bulged and her lips parted in protest. She didn't think I could do it. I had to pry the microphone out of her hand.

"Uh…hi…uh…everyone," I began nervously.

"We love you, Dancing Queen!" Someone yelled followed by more applause and cheers. Then the crowd grew quiet again. I looked out on the sea of faces staring up at me waiting to hear something profound. Nothing profound was coming to me. A weight of doubt sat in the pit of my belly. I thought I might vomit.

Then I found Will smiling at me. 'You can do this,' he mouthed. He was right. I *could* do this. What was I so afraid of? I took a deep breath and said, "I want to thank all of you for your votes, but more importantly, I want to thank you for the confidence you've given me. I've never been cool, or popular, or beautiful and you've made me feel like all those things tonight. Congratulations to the other four nominees, Sophie, Caroline, Hayley, and," I paused dramatically then added, "Lauren," noticeably leaving off the *DeHaven*.

Lauren DeHaven momentarily lost her cool and angrily crossed her arms. I could almost see steam seeping out of her ears as she glared at me and Sasha.

When the speech ended and I left the stage, I had never been so relieved in my life. After Poe and I danced the king and queen dance, I found Will and convinced him we should go. It had been a perfect evening so far, and I wanted to leave before anything changed.

***

Somehow the spring recital at Ms. Alexander's studio kinda snuck up on me. Not to say I wasn't prepared. It's just that usually I spent the two weeks before the show doing publicity. I traveled to local public schools and performed solo excerpts from the show. I hoped maybe there was a younger version of myself sitting in the audience who I could inspire to lead a life of dance. That year I didn't do my little tour. Because of the prospect of DiRisio, it was likely my last performance with the studio so Ms. Alexander wanted it to be a complete surprise. I had three solos that even the other members of the cast had never seen before.

In Ms. Alexander's studio, we usually stayed away from the classic ballets like, Cinderella, Sleeping Beauty, and Romeo and Juliet. When Ms. Alexander was in her prime, she never got cast in those lead parts. She said American audiences didn't want to see a Japanese Cinderella, Princess Aurora or Juliet. She didn't want me to go through the same struggles she did. So, most of our performances were her original creations. And they were beautiful. We did still have to do the Nutcracker every year. It was just expected. But she braved the complaints and cast me as Clara anyway.

I kinda felt like this year's show was a tribute to me. It began with the entire cast performing a series of rigid movements while wearing the same style drab taupe costume. Then I entered wearing a stunning rose colored tutu performing the same choreography except with more fluidity. I'm shunned and no one will even look at me or acknowledge my existence. Enter the leading man, who joins me in my unique interpretation of love and dance. For this part, I pretended it was Will on stage with me gently lifting me to new heights of self expression.

Over the course of two acts, my character transforms the entire stage into one of color. Not only do the other cast members look at me, but I proceed to lead them in a number filled with dramatic leaps and spectacular turn sequences. In the end, it's clear that I finally belong.

Will bought me so many flowers that I could barely see to walk. As soon as I entered the parking lot, I heard clapping. I lowered the flowers and saw that there were at least fifty Bridgeton students holding flowers for me and signs with my name. Apparently, Will had organized a group of students to come and support me. It was the first time my fellow students had ever seen me dance…well, without a table that is.

For a while, everything was right in my universe. I was on top at the studio, I was popular at school, and most importantly, I was loved by Will. But, oh, how quickly things can change.

***

"What the hell is this?" Sasha said a week later as she held a piece of paper in her hand. I mentally went through all the quizzes and tests I'd had in the past couple of days and I really didn't think I had failed any. I hadn't gotten my Spanish test back, but I was pretty sure I'd aced it. I had no idea why Sasha was angry with me.

"Sasha, I haven't failed any test, I swear," I pleaded with her.

"You have no idea what I'm talking about?" she asked, softening a little.

"No."

"Have you checked the message board?"

"No," I said as she started to drag me to the main office.

When we got there, she pointed to the bulletin board and said, "Read that." I almost couldn't believe my eyes. I had to read it three times and each time my heart beat faster and faster and louder and louder until it pounded in my ears. I had been summoned before the honor council.

Chapter 21:
Four Words

As student body president, Sasha received a special notice saying she had to sit on the council. I could understand her anxiety. She had to decide whether or not to expel her sister from school.

"Honestly, did you cheat?" I never, ever thought I'd have to hear those four words from my sister. "Please tell me you didn't cheat on something."

"Sasha, I have no idea what this is about. Of course, I didn't cheat. Have you seen my grades?"

Sasha stared at me for a while trying to gauge the veracity of my words. She must have decided to believe me because she said, "Well, if you didn't cheat, what is -," she paused. "Those bitches!" she yelled before storming off.

"What's this about an honor trial?" Will asked when

he met me at the tree for lunch; the tree that used to be a special place for me and Sasha.

"I didn't cheat, Will. You gotta believe me." Will hugged.

"Of course, I believe you. Everyone does. The entire school is behind you on this one." Will brushed a strand of hair away from my face then handed me a sandwich. "They're gonna have to have some extreme amount of evidence against you," he said sitting on the ground and taking out his lunch of three turkey club sandwiches, three bottles of chocolate milk and three bags of Doritos. My stomach churned either from the thought of Will wolfing down all that food or the thought of my integrity being publicly challenged.

"I can't eat this," I said, sitting down and handing him my sandwich.

"Well, I can't eat it. I already have three," he said with his mouth full. I shook my head and unwrapped the sandwich. "So, do you know who brought up the charges?"

"I'll give you one guess."

He nodded, knowing exactly who I was talking about. "They're not through with you, with us. They know whatever they do to you hurts me as well." Will leaned over and kissed me on the cheek. I stared down at my turkey sandwich dejectedly. "Don't worry, angel. Their other plans failed, this one will too."

I wished I shared Will's confidence on the matter, but I couldn't. My whole time at Bridgeton, I had never seen an

honor trial turn out well. Every single one resulted in
expulsion.

After sorting through the rumor mill, Sasha and I
found out that David Winthrop had been caught cheating on
an exam and, for some reason, he implicated me as well. We
knew the Bitch Brigade had put him up to it. I still had no
idea what kind of proof he could have against me.

The night before the trial, I sat wrapped in Will's arms
on his living room couch. We both stared blankly at the TV.
Will hadn't said a word in over an hour. I could tell
something bothered him. I had already asked him twice if he
wanted to talk and both times he just shrugged and kept
staring at the TV. Finally, he turned it off and said, "What is
it with you and David?"

"What? What are you talking about?" I asked as I sat
up.

"Do you still have feelings for him?"

"What? How...I...why...still?" I stuttered in shock.
How could he think that?

"Cause if you want to be with him -"

"Will, what are you talking about?" I asked, finally
able to spit out a coherent sentence.

"Look, I knew before I even asked you out that you
had a crush on him. I was hoping you'd get over it or
something, but I don't think you have. I see the way you look
at him. And then the night I propose, you go to his house!
And now, he's implicating you in this cheating thing. I just

don't know what's going on."

So, he was jealous of David. "Where is this coming from? I thought you believed me."

"I did...I do...I don't know what to believe." Will stood up and ran his fingers through his golden hair. "Brandon says he saw you and David in the physics lab after school being...intimate," he said as he paced the floor.

"What! Who the heck is Brandon?"

"He's the small forward on the team. Look, who he is doesn't matter. What he saw, does. Were you with David?"

"Will!" I said shocked he'd believe such a thing.

"Cause I've been completely honest with you. I know I'm no saint, but at least I've told you the truth. If you just tell me the truth, I can forgive you and we can move on. Unless, of course, you really want David, in which case - "

"Will, can't you see what's happening? It's the Bitch Brigade again. They probably put Brandon up to this. They're trying to sow seeds of doubt between us. They're still trying to break us up." I stood up and walked over to him. I grabbed his hands and said, "You have every right to be concerned. For a long time, I did have a crush on David, but that was before I really knew him or you. That was before I knew myself and what I wanted."

Will stared down at our hands entwined together. He wasn't convinced. I led him back to the couch and sat him down. "And what I want," I said as I lifted his head up to stare into his sweet blue eyes, "is you." I kissed him gently on the lips. He didn't return it. "Please, believe me," I whispered as I continued kissing him. "I don't think I can get through this thing without you." He looked down again and shook his head like he couldn't believe me. I sat on top of him straddling him with my legs. I cupped his face in my hands, looked him in the eyes and said, "Will, I love you."

Will had been waiting to hear those four words from me for weeks. Something in him snapped and he kissed me like never before. He wrapped his arms around my waist and lowered me onto the couch as he hovered above me. His kisses were slow and deep and warm and perfect and each one sent a shiver of delight down my spine. Each caress of his lips and thrust of his tongue was a testimony to the emotional void I had filled in his life.

Will sat up and pulled his shirt off. His chiseled porcelain body made me want to weep with expectation and desire. Then he laid on top of me and whispered, "I love you."

"I know," I said as I ran my fingers up and down the center of his back.

"I think I fell in love with you the first time I saw you," he added as he stared at me asking with his eyes if I was really ready for this step we were about to take. I responded by unbuttoning his pants. "Are you sure?" he asked. I nodded. Will reached in his back pocket, pulled out a small plastic package and then, believe it or not, the phone rang. Both of us let out grunts of frustration as Will reached over me and grabbed the phone. "Hold that thought," he said with a smile before he put the phone to his ear hoping we would be able to resume shortly. But I could tell within a few seconds by the change in Will's face that wasn't going to happen. He crawled off of me and stood up. I can't repeat exactly what he said because I don't like profanity, but I will say that he literally picked up the phone and threw it across the room breaking two picture frames and a vase.

"What's wrong?" I asked as I backed away from him a little on the couch.

"I'm sorry. I didn't mean to scare you." Will buttoned his pants then put on his shirt. "My sister got arrested. Drunk driving. I have to go bail her out of jail."

"Oh, my God!"

"She's such an...idiot. I can't wait till I'm out of her house." Will put on his sneakers while simultaneously looking for his keys. I just sat there not knowing whether I should offer to go with him or wait or what. "I should just leave her dumb ass in jail!"

"Don't say that, Will. She's your sister and, even with all her faults, you love her. Deep down you know you'd do anything for her. I know I would for *my* sister." I didn't know how true those words were until the next day at the trial.

Chapter 22:

Caught in the Noose 2

I opted for an open trial in front of the school. Sasha
tried to convince me to go with a closed trial with just
Headmaster Collins and my accuser, but I knew I had
nothing to hide. I wanted the whole school to see David and
the Bitch Brigade fail.

The trial took place in Dardem Hall. The five
members of the honor council, which included my sister, sat
behind the bench in the middle of the stage. Then I sat on the
left and David on the right. My fingers trembled as I
watched the student body file in. I sat on my hands to keep
them still.

I noticed a couple of students had actually made
posters proclaiming my innocence. It comforted me

somewhat, knowing so many people were on my side. That comfort slipped away when I saw Ashley, Brittany, and Lauren DeHaven strut to the front of Dardem Hall. They each gave me an evil grin as they took their seats. I found Will in the audience and felt a surge of pride and calm as he mouthed the words "I love you" before taking his seat.

Headmaster Collins called the meeting to order and explained why the procedure was necessary.

"Mr. Winthrop has accused Ms. Garrison of cheating on a test and conspiracy to hide this dishonorable conduct. They will each have five minutes to present their version of events after which the honor council will adjourn to make their decision. Mr. Winthrop, please begin."

"Headmaster Collins, I would just like to say that I admit to cheating on several occasions during my education here at Bridgeton. I apologize for my deplorable behavior. I no longer want to bring reproach upon this school, and I want to make sure that the remaining students are the honest trustworthy individuals that deserve a Bridgeton diploma." David spoke with such sincerity and remorse he almost convinced me he was telling the truth; until he began the rest of his speech. "The defendant is not one of these individuals. On January 15th, I found the defendant crying in the stairwell of the Chesterfield building. I approached her and asked what was wrong. She said she was extremely stressed and tired and she hadn't had time to study for her Spanish test. I felt sorry for her and offered to help. I'd just taken the test the period before, so I knew what questions were on it. I wrote the questions down and gave them to her. She later aced the test."

"Winthrop is a lying, punk-ass, prick!" a boy in the audience yelled. My sentiments exactly.

"Mr. Haden, please remove that young man from the building," Headmaster Collins said. "Continue, Mr. Winthrop."

I started to feel supremely confident as I knew he'd never be able to prove this. I'd be the first student ever to go through an honor trial and come out victorious. I crossed my legs and sat back in my chair as a teacher wheeled out a TV on a cart.

"After the cheating incident," David continued, "I knew I had her right where I wanted her. I began to ask her for favors, sexual favors, and if she refused I threatened to reveal her secret and get her expelled." David walked over to the TV and turned it on. "What she didn't know is that I keep a video camera in my bedroom and I taped one of our encounters. What you're about to see is extremely incriminating towards me. But I apologize for my actions and I accept my expulsion. I just want to see that justice is served for everyone." I sat up in my seat. I didn't know who this could be on the video because it sure wasn't me. Sasha gave me a panicked look. I shrugged in confusion.

A grainy, poorly lit tape with awful sound began to play and, sure enough, there was David and someone who looked like me arguing about this being the last time. But it wasn't me. I knew it wasn't me. I mean, I knew I had been in David's house before. Everyone knew that. There were pictures. But I really didn't remember having this conversation. Could I have done this when I was drunk? The girl in the video didn't appear drunk. What the hell was going on?

"*I can't do this anymore. I don't care if you get me expelled*," the girl in the video said.

"*I don't think you mean that. What would your sister say? This is the only way. I promise no one will ever find out as long as you give me what I want.*"

"*Look, I'll pay you. I'll give you money. Just don't -* "

"*You know that's not what I want.*" David approached the girl in the video, undid her ponytail and tossed the pink scrunchie to the side; a pink scrunchie that looked remarkably like mine. I touched the back of my head and, sure enough, I was wearing my favorite pink scrunchie with the tutus on it.

David ran his fingers through her hair then he kissed her neck. I cringed. Three months ago, I would've given anything to have David Winthrop touch me like that. But now, the thought of him coming near me turned my stomach. David grabbed her neck forcefully and said, "*Now, are you gonna be a good girl and cooperate? Or do I need to call Headmaster Collins?*"

The girl in the video looked down and started unbuttoning her shirt. Then it hit me.

"Shut it off!" I yelled, bolting out of my chair. The audience gasped. Sasha started crying hysterically. To everyone else, my outburst and her crying seemed like my admission of guilt. The devotion of my supporters plummeted, as the signs proclaiming my innocence inched down and disappeared from sight. A chilling silence fell over the crowd.

I looked out over the auditorium and saw the Bitch Brigade sitting in the front row smiling. They were enjoying my torment. I so wanted to expose them for what they really were. I wanted to spit out everything they had done to people at Bridgeton and explain what really took place in that video. But I knew I couldn't do that. Our 'Get Out of Venton Heights' plan depended on what I chose to do next.

I turned my focus away from the Bitch Brigade and found Will's ashen white face. I couldn't tell whether he wanted to vomit or cry or both. This had to feel like the ultimate betrayal to him, after I had just assured him last night that nothing happened between me and David.

I looked over at Sasha, who held her face in her hands as her shoulders shook with sobs. And though I loved them both, I knew what I had to do. And I had to do it soon. Any second, someone could have realized the girl in the video was Sasha and not me.

"Young lady, do you have something to say?" Headmaster Collins barked at me.

I nodded as I wiped my sweaty hands on my green plaid skirt. Then I shrugged with doubt. Where would I find the courage to take the blame for my sister's cheating? What would Will think of me? The answers really didn't matter. I had to do it. I looked to Will, then Sasha, then Will. I mouthed "I'm sorry" to Will then said to Headmaster Collins, "I'm guilty." It wasn't a complete lie. I did feel guilty. I felt guilty for ever lusting after that sleaze David Winthrop especially while I was with Will. And I felt guilty for what my sister had apparently been driven to do. I should have paid more attention to her. I should have realized no one could work as hard as she did without breaking at some point.

Sasha screamed 'no' and ran over to me.

"Don't do this," she sobbed as she embraced me. "I can fix it. Let me fix it. It's all my fault. I'm sorry."

Headmaster Collins said something about me being expelled from school and ordered me to leave campus immediately, but Sasha wouldn't let me go. They had to pull her off of me as she yelled, "No, not my sister, please, no!"

I wasn't even allowed time to clean out my locker. Mr. Hayden, the assistant head of school, escorted me off campus. As the main gate slammed shut behind me, so did all my dreams for a bright future.

Chapter 23:
Trapped

Believe it or not, I didn't cry. Maybe the shock of the situation had temporarily clogged my tear ducts. Or, maybe, I thought I'd dreamt the whole thing. It didn't really happen. I dreamt it. I tried to convince myself as I stood on the corner and looked at my school. Then, I looked down at my ballet pink tights and my green plaid skirt. Why did I wear these tights? Oh, yeah, I'd decided to take a page out of Will's book. I thought they'd be good luck. So much for that. I had to breathe deeply to keep from hyperventilating. I turned my back to Bridgeton, my past, my former school, and I walked.

I rationalized the situation as I found my way to the bus stop. Okay, I was expelled from Bridgeton, but it wasn't that bad, right. I wanted to be a dancer. I didn't need to graduate from Bridgeton in order to be a dancer. But Sasha, yes, she needed a Bridgeton diploma in order to go to Princeton. So, yes, I did the right thing. I couldn't let anyone find out it was her on that tape.

So, why did I feel so awful? I did the right thing. I did the right thing. No matter how many times I said it, it didn't feel right. No one at Bridgeton would ever look at me the same, including Will. I had to talk to him. Maybe if I told him the truth...no, I couldn't do that. He'd tell Headmaster Collins and get Sasha expelled. Maybe if I just told him that I was sorry and I loved him, maybe he'd forgive me.

I found a payphone and dialed his cell number.

"Maddox," he answered.

"Will, baby, please listen to - "

"I feel like an idiot. You're a whore and I never want to see you again." Then he hung up on me.

The full impact of the trial, Bridgeton, losing Will and saving Sasha didn't hit until I sat on my bed at home. I had sacrificed my education, my boyfriend, and my future.

So, then, I cried. I cried painful, violent, heart-twisting tears. I cried until I could cry no more; until my throat sealed dry and tight and my eyes wouldn't stay open of their own volition. Then sleep came to swallow me whole, but brought me no relief since I dreamt of Will. Even in my dream, he didn't want me anymore.

"Why did you do it?" Sasha asked when she came home and woke me from my fitful slumber.

"Why did *I* do it?" I asked, sitting up and rubbing the

sleep out of my red swollen eyes. "I didn't have a choice. I couldn't let them find out it was you. You would've had your acceptance to Princeton revoked." Sasha sat down on the bed and placed her face in her hands.

"I ruined your life, didn't I?"

"How could you cheat, Sasha? How could you risk everything on a stupid little Spanish test?" For the first time, the tables had turned. It wasn't Sasha scolding me for saying something stupid or failing a test. This time, I reprimanded her.

"I don't know how it happened. It was a moment of weakness. I was really stressed out and I didn't have time to study and I just thought of it as a little study aid." Sasha buried her face in her hands and cried. It seemed like her eyes hadn't healed since her last breakdown.

"And then you slept with him to cover it up?"

"I would've done anything to protect us from something like this. I never thought you'd get dragged into it. I still don't know why he took you down instead of me." Sasha wiped tears from her eyes and tried to gain some composure.

"Maybe he really can't tell us apart," I said, even though I knew the real reason. Since I had just shown the entire Bridgeton community what I looked like in my underwear, I'm sure people easily imagined I'd do something as sleazy as sleep with David to cover up an honor violation. No one would even believe Sasha could do such a thing. By accusing me instead of Sasha, the Bitch Brigade finally got their revenge. They had me right where they wanted. They knew no matter what I did, I would lose. If I didn't take the blame and let my sister get expelled, I would've felt just as bad.

"What are we gonna do?" she asked, flopping backwards on her bed. "I can't let you take the fall for me."

"What's done is done. It's over." I sighed.

"No, don't say that. I can fix this. Maybe I can talk to David and get him to take it all back." She stood up excitedly as a plan started to form in her mind.

"It doesn't matter. I already confessed. Even if David took it back, I still committed an honor violation by saying I cheated when I didn't." She sat back down and mulled this over. Out of the corner of my eye I saw a roach making its way across our bedroom wall. A surge of anger flowed through me. Suddenly, I hated those roaches as much as Sasha, maybe more. It was this place, this apartment, this neighborhood, these roaches, that had put us in the position we were now in. Sasha's determination to make a better life for us had forced her into a dead end path for which there was no escape. We were trapped. I picked up a lamp and flung it against the wall, demolishing the roach and the lamp.

"What are you doing?" Sasha yelled, as she covered her head with her arms.

"It's better this way. You deserve Princeton. You've worked too hard for anything less. At least one of us needs to get out of here." Sasha came over to my bed and hugged me.

"I'll never leave you behind. I'll figure something

out."

      It *was* better this way I decided. I wasn't as smart as Sasha. She deserved her shot at an Ivy League education. She shouldn't have that taken away from her because of one moment of weakness. I, on the other hand, had options. I just wanted to dance. I didn't need a high school diploma for that. Or so I thought.

Chapter 24:
Sweet Release

"What the hell were you thinking?" my mother asked, slamming a jar of peanut butter on the counter. I had just given her a short summary of the honor trial, leaving out the minor detail that I was completely innocent. If she knew the truth, she'd take matters into her own hands and talk to Headmaster Collins herself.

"I guess I wasn't really thinking." I hung my head low afraid of making eye contact with her. One look at me and she'd see I was lying.

"Damn straight you weren't. Cheating? And on a Spanish test? Sonya, that's just not like you. You're fluent in Spanish." My mother fell silent for a moment as she went back to preparing her lunch for work. I thought maybe she was starting to put things together. My pulse quickened. What if she figured out the truth on her own? But then she said, "I bet it was because of dance. I bet you were so busy

practicing that you didn't have time to study so you felt you
had to cheat."

I nodded numbly. I hated that she blamed it on dance,
but what could I say. I swallowed my pride and accepted I
would just have to let her think that. It was the only way
Sasha could go to Princeton.

My mother put her peanut butter and jelly sandwich
into a baggie then crammed it into her purse. Without another
word, she headed to the door on her way to the hospital for a
twelve hour shift. Before leaving she paused and said, "I'm so
disappointed in you. Why can't you be more like Sasha?"

Angry tears stung behind my eyes, but I remained
strong. As long as I got into DiRisio, everything would be
okay. In a few months, I'd be living in Rome and starting my
fantastic, limitless future. Then my mother wouldn't see me
as a failure anymore. All would be forgotten.

Another part of my determination to get into DiRisio
could have been the fact that I knew Will would be in Rome.
Maybe a part of me believed that we could rekindle our
relationship in a foreign, romantic city.

I missed him so much. I hadn't seen or spoken to him
since the honor trial. He never called or came to the studio or
showed any kind of sign that he wanted to ever see or speak
to me again. I couldn't blame him. I would've been
devastated if I had seen a video of him having sex with
someone else. Although a part of me wished that he'd
realize it wasn't me. I wished somehow he could look inside
his heart and realize that I'd always be true to him.

I tried to call him every day from different numbers, but he always hung up once he heard my voice. Sometimes I imagined he was watching me through the window like he used to before we knew each other. I thought I saw him walk past the studio one day and I ran out after him. But once I got outside, he was nowhere to be found. Finally, three days before the audition, I decided I couldn't take it anymore and I went to his house.

"What are you doing here?" he asked when he opened the door. Surprisingly, he seemed more shocked than angry.

"I needed to see you. I need to hear your voice. I need *you*." Will looked over his shoulder. "Is Julia home?" I asked.

"No, she's...um doing community service. Part of her probation for the DUI."

"Can I come in?"

"Uhh...I don't think that's a good idea." Will stepped through the door and closed it behind him. Without thinking, I lunged forward and hugged him tightly. He didn't return the embrace. "I'm so sorry, I hurt you, Will. I'll do anything if you just forgive me. I love you." My tears soaked his shirt. Will buried his face in my hair. He pulled away from me and gently wiped my tears with his fingertips. I thought for a moment I had won him back. But then, the door opened and the devil herself walked through.

"Will? What are you - ...Oh, it's you," Ashley Carter sneered. She possessively wrapped her arms around Will's waist and said, "Are you crying again? I swear to God you have absolutely no backbone whatsoever." She let go of

Will's waist and took a step forward causing me to step back. "You were such an easy target," she said blowing her rum laden breath in my face. Or it could have been whiskey, vodka or tequila. How should I know? But I did know I was tired of being a target. I no longer wanted to be the victim. I needed to stand up for myself and fight back.

My first punch landed right below her left eye and sent her reeling to the ground. I jumped on top of her and continued my assault on her face. I never imagined what a sweet release it would be to feel my fist make contact with her white, rich, snotty, over-privileged face.

Will came behind me and lifted me up as Ashley tried to stand and retreat. He restrained my arms preventing me from throwing another punch, but he failed to realize my legs were even more of a weapon. I kicked and flailed my legs landing several more blows to her face.

"My nose! I think she broke my nose!" she cried, tears streaming down her face.

"Ashley, get in the house!" Will yelled, still restraining me. Ashley ran inside, flinging the door shut behind her.

"Who's crying now, bitch?" I screamed after her. "Let me go, Will. Let me go." I scrambled free and lunged for the door, but he grabbed me again.

"What has gotten into you?" he asked, pulling me away from his front door and toward the street.

"What's gotten into *me*? What's gotten into *you*?" I panted using all my strength to escape his grasp. "How could you go back to her? After all she did to me, how could you?" I shoved him so hard he stumbled backward a little. "You're such a hypocrite. I hate you. I hate you!" I punched him in the chest over and over.

Will grabbed my wrists and pulled me to him. He stared deep into my eyes and breathed in sharply like he wanted to say something, but decided against it. He looked at his house then at me. Then he closed his eyes, released me, and said, "I think you should go."

The fire that grew inside me from watching Ashley with my man blazed as I stormed away from Will's house.

The next thing I knew I was on Emmaline Graham's doorstep. It was time we had a little chat.

Chapter 25:
Ballerina Girl

Somehow, I had to accept the fact that Will and I were over. He was only my *first* boyfriend. There would be other boys, right? Probably not. I don't know why, but for some reason men never really showed an interest in me. I never got cat calls when I walked through Venton Heights and besides Will, no boy had ever asked me out. From fifth to eighth grade, Tyrell Fitts gave me cards on Valentine's Day and my birthday, but other than that he barely spoke to me. I didn't even think he knew my name. On the few occasions he did talk to me, he called me Ballerina Girl. In any case, at the end of eighth grade, when LaPorscha got pregnant with his baby, the cards stopped. I guess he figured it wasn't right to send one woman cards when another was about to have his child.

Maybe I was just too weird. Maybe I just bored

people too much with all my talk of dance and Russian ballerinas. I shouldn't have even worried about it. I should've just been happy that I didn't get hit on by strange men all the time. I should have realized how lucky I was in that regard.

"Hey pretty lady," a man said to me as I was walking home one night. I ignored him and kept walking. Once again I had missed all the buses and Sasha was at a party or something. I wasn't quite sure. It was hard for me to keep up with her these days. With graduation a week away, I guess she was really busy.

"Don't be so stuck up. I just wanna talk to ya. I thought I knew all the pretty ladies 'round here." An unshaven man of about thirty with missing teeth stepped in front of me forcing me to stop. "I'm Rayshon," he said leaning in closer. His breath smelled like a mixture of marijuana and alcohol. It was foul. I tried to step around him, but he blocked my path. "Ain't you gonna tell me yo name before you go?" I turned and walked in the other direction. In three steps he was in front of me again.

I looked around into the darkness of my neighborhood. My apartment was still two blocks away and no one was outside. Why did I keep walking through this place alone and at night? Why didn't I just stay the night at the studio?

I turned again and walked quickly towards my apartment. My heart raced and I could feel a lump developing in my throat soon to be followed by uncontrollable tears. Rayshon grabbed my arm and said, "I just wanna talk to ya. Where ya goin'?"

"Let go of me!" I yelled as I flung my dance bag at him with all my might. Rayshon gripped me tighter. I closed my eyes and tried to squirm away from him. Then I heard a click and Rayshon instantly let go of me.

"The only reason you're not dead already is because I don't want to get blood on my friend," Tyrell said calmly as he pointed a gun at Rayshon's temple.

"Yo, Boo Man, I-"

"Shut up." Tyrell pushed Rayshon away from me with the barrel of his gun. "This is how this is going to work. You are never gonna touch her again. You're never gonna look at her or even speak her name. If you do, I'll go to your home, kill your mother, your father, your grandmother, your aunts, uncles and cousins," he said in an eerie matter of fact manner. "But I won't stop there. I'll wait a few years. Let your children have children. I'll kill them. Then I'll come for you. Do I make myself clear?" My assailant nodded his head furiously. I think he might have wet his pants. "Get out of here before I change my mind and empty my clip into the side of your head right now." After Rayshon scurried away, Tyrell said to me, "You alright, Ballerina Girl?" I didn't respond. I was in shock. Tyrell tucked his gun into the back of his pants then held out his arms to me. I buried my face in his chest and tried to gain control of my breathing. "I'm sorry I didn't get here sooner," he said as he held me securely to him.

***

"Thank you, Tyrell," I said as I drank a cup of tea at my kitchen table. He had walked me back to my apartment and waited for me as I took a shower. He wanted to make sure I felt safe before he left.

"I'm glad I was there. I hate to think what could have happened. I can't believe he would try something like that. Rayshon should know better than to mess with you."

"Why?"

"Because I said so." I gave Tyrell a confused look. I didn't know what he was talking about. I didn't even know Rayshon before tonight. How would he know not to mess with me? "Every guy around here knows not to touch my Ballerina Girl."

"Excuse me?" I asked nearly choking on a sip of tea.

"Don't be mad at me. I just wanted to keep you safe."

"I'm not mad. At least, I think I'm not mad. I'm just confused. Did you do the same for Sasha?"

"Sasha?" Tyrell laughed a little. "Trust me, Sasha can take care of herself. But you, you're different." Tyrell took out his gun and started fiddling with it nervously. My eyes grew large. I had never seen a gun up close before tonight. He noticed my discomfort and quickly put it away again. Tyrell cleared his throat, looked down and said, "You're like this rare, precious, beautiful, flower growing with a bunch of weeds. I just wanted to protect you."

"So you told every boy in the neighborhood to stay away from me? That's why I've never been asked to a dance or to dinner or to a movie or anything? All this time I thought something was wrong with me."

"Nothing's wrong with you. You're perfect." I looked down into my cup. I took a spoon and started stirring even though there was no sugar in it. I never knew Tyrell felt this way. "I didn't mean for it to seem like something was wrong with you. I just felt no one around here was good enough for you."

"Tyrell, what are you trying to say?" Tyrell reached across the table and clasped my hands in his.

"I'm saying that you're too good for this apartment, for this neighborhood, for the people in this neighborhood...even for me. You're too good for me." I was speechless. "I've had a thing for you since fifth grade, but I care for you too much to see you get attached to anything or anyone in this place. You deserve better."

"Tyrell, I-"

"Aren't you with Wonderbread now?" he asked, trying to change the subject somewhat. He let go of my hands and leaned back in his chair.

"What?"

"Wonderbread. White Will. He plays ball with us down on Fifth Street sometimes. That's what we call him on the court."

"Oh, Will. We...he...we're not together anymore, I guess."

"What did he do to you?" he asked protectively as he sat upright in his chair.

"No, he didn't…it's not…he thinks…well, to use his words exactly, I'm a whore and he never wants to see me again."

Tyrell laughed. "I barely know you and I know that's not true. Maybe he's not good enough for you after all."

A strange feeling roused in me toward Tyrell. He wasn't especially attractive. Nothing really stood out about him except a dimple in his left cheek so deep you could almost see it when he wasn't even smiling. Other than that he looked just like five or six other black teenagers in Venton Heights: tall, dark, and athletic. But something about his demeanor made him completely irresistible to the girls in the neighborhood. Maybe his charisma made him stand out or the amount of power he wielded even with people twice his age.

In any case, I saw him in a new light. Despite his façade, he was sweet and he cared about me. He had protected me in Venton Heights for years without my even realizing it. He barely knew me, but he knew I wouldn't cheat on Will. Why didn't Will see that? Maybe Will *wasn't* the one. Maybe Tyrell was. I mean, I let Tyrell into my roach infested apartment and I didn't feel a tinge of shame. I knew Tyrell understood. Tyrell lived like me. Will would never have that understanding. He would never know what it was like to grow up in a place like this. Maybe I needed someone like Tyrell.

"So what are you gonna do about it?"

"About what?"

"Word on the street is you got kicked out of the fancy

white school for cheating."

Great. Even Tyrell had heard about it. I nodded and took a sip of my tea.

"Well, what are you gonna do about it? I know you didn't cheat. You're not like that. And the girl I know who has spent the last eight years cleaning a dance studio in exchange for lessons isn't one that gives up so easily. You're stronger than you think." When I didn't respond, he added, "How are you gonna clear your rep and get your man back?"

I stared into the cup as if the answer was swimming around my bitter, sugarless cup of tea. Then a smile formed on my lips when I thought about how I'd already showed my strength, right on Ashley's face. Tyrell was right. I was strong.

"You're right. I didn't cheat. I was set up."

"You got proof?"

I shook my head. "Not really. I mean, I know who did it and there's this girl named Emmaline who will corroborate how evil these girls are. It took me hours to convince her to talk at all. But even with Emmaline it's still our word against theirs."

Tyrell nodded. "I see how it is. You want me to take 'em out?"

I giggled nervously, but I really wasn't sure if he was joking or not.

"I better get going," Tyrell said after looking at his

watch. He stood up from the table and put on his huge leather jacket.

"Tyrell," I said, leaping from my chair. "You can stay...if you want." I don't know what possessed me to say this. I was confused and lonely and scared and I wanted someone. I wanted to feel loved.

Tyrell approached me slowly. He stared into my eyes. He had beautiful eyes. His eyelashes were so long and dark they would make any woman jealous. He reached out his hand and traced the side of my neck from my ear to my collarbone with his fingertips. Then he cupped my face in his hands and brought his thick luscious lips towards me. But at the last second, he turned his face and kissed me tenderly on the cheek. Then he whispered, "Good night, Ballerina Girl."

Chapter 26:
The Audition

The night before my audition, I couldn't sleep. I couldn't turn my mind off. Every time I closed my eyes I saw images, Bridgeton, Headmaster Collins, Sasha, David Winthrop, Ashley, Ms. Alexander, Tyrell and Will. The most traumatic events of my life just kept replaying on this torturous continuous loop in my head. The image that appeared most - Will. No matter how hard I tried, I couldn't purge him from my mind. I still loved him.

I rolled over and looked at the clock. Three a.m. In six hours, I'd be standing in front of three people who held my future in their hands. A flutter of nerves filled my stomach. I needed to talk to someone. I needed reassurance. I leaned up on one arm and peered over at Sasha's bed. She wasn't there. Three o'clock in the morning and she wasn't home. I jumped out of bed and ran to my mother's room.

"Mom, Sasha's not here!" I said, bursting through the door.

"What?" she groaned sleepily.

"Sasha's missing. I think we should call the police."

"She's not missing." My mother yawned. "She called me at work. Said she's spending the night with someone named Lauren."

"Lauren? Lauren who?" My mother didn't answer. I think she'd fallen back asleep just that quickly. "Mom, do you remember a last name?" I asked, shaking her. "Did she say a last name? Was it DeHaven, Rovick, Holloway, Smith?"

"Huh?"

"Mom, this is important. Did she say a last name?"

"Who?"

"Sasha!"

"No, she just said Laura or something."

"Laura? Mom, try to think. Did she say Lauren or Laura?" My mother responded with loud snoring.

I gave up trying to jog the sleep out of my mother's memory and went back to my room even more agitated than before. Where was my sister the night before my big audition? Why wasn't she here supporting and comforting me? Was it even possible that she would be with Lauren DeHaven? No, that wasn't possible. My mother had gotten the names confused. Sasha had spent the night over Laura's house. But no one named Laura went to Bridgeton.

Needless to say, I didn't get much sleep that night. Before I knew it, my alarm clock blared in my ears. Since I didn't have to share bathroom time with my missing sister, I took a long leisurely shower. Still being subconsciously influenced by Will's superstition, I didn't want to wear my pink scrunchie or pink ballet tights thinking they were bad luck. Instead, I opted for a black scrunchie and black tights. I went with a stylish maroon leotard and maroon leg warmers to offset the black.

On the bus ride to the audition, I thought about the Bitch Brigade and all they had done to me. But I was still here and I still had a chance to win. As determined as they were to break me that's how determined I was to succeed. This new found strength stayed with me throughout the audition. I held my head high and projected a confidence and grace that made me stand apart from the four other applicants. I could feel the judges staring at me and nodding their approval as we did the fundamental part of the audition. For all intents and purposes, I might as well have been the only one on stage as we performed the combinations and exercises that had been taught to us just minutes before.

When the time came to perform my solo, I struck my opening position in front of the three judges. As the Chopin nocturne began, I blocked out the outside world and let the music move me. I was glad I chose such a slow, smooth, and beautiful song for my first piece. It allowed me to glide and float across the floor becoming the epitome of exquisite. The Chopin song contrasted perfectly against the Stravinsky symphony of my second number. In this dynamic piece, I jumped and leapt and executed the choreography with such precision that I even surprised myself.

I danced better than I ever had before. I think something inside me knew that this was my last hope. Not only was my technique flawless throughout each piece, but I put so much emotion into every move that I even shocked myself.

"That was remarkable," the tall blond judge said as she clasped her hands in front of her excitedly.

"The best we've seen today," said another judge. He had dark hair and a moustache and seemed a bit overweight to be a dancer. I guess he could've been a choreographer. "Maybe the best we've seen on the east coast. I'm seriously considering borrowing your entire solo for the company's next performance. Of course, we'll give you full credit."

"Thank you!" I beamed. I couldn't begin to imagine my name in the DiRisio Ballet Company's program as a contributing choreographer. What a dream come true!

Just then, a man entered the room and handed the blond judge a manila envelope. She read through it then handed it to the other two judges. They started shuffling papers and exchanging awkward glances. Two of them exchanged words in Italian then silence. My heart started racing. Finally, the third judge, a man with a French accent said, "The DiRisio Academy is a world class dance instruction facility. Only four academy graduates per year are asked to join the DiRisio Ballet Company. Admission into the academy and the company is extremely competitive."

I smiled and nodded not knowing exactly where he

was going with his little speech. "You are skilled enough even now to gain admittance into the company. Unfortunately, there is not a free spot with the company right now. We are just looking to fill three positions in the academy." He sighed then looked down at the file again. "The academy," he added, "not only provides dance instruction, but also academic instruction. It is a school." My stomach tightened into a knot. "We have to be aware of what message we send when we accept a new student." Oh God, I knew where the speech headed. "While we know you are obviously an amazing and accomplished dancer we cannot accept you. We've received your transcript from Bridgeton and apparently you were dismissed for an honor violation."

I didn't hear anything after that. My breath caught in my throat and I had to remind myself to tell my lungs to do their job. My world came crashing down. It was over. Everything was over.

Chapter 27:
The Truth

I didn't know how I made it home that day. I had just danced an audition worthy of the Joffrey Ballet, but after that rejection I had trouble making my legs work. They wouldn't obey simple commands. It took all of my brain power to tell each leg to take another step forward. I had to concentrate on not collapsing. I didn't even have the brain power to find the correct bus to take home, so I focused on one step at a time until I made it back to Venton Heights.

Venton Heights: the place where I'd probably live for the rest of my life. I could teach some extra classes at the studio to earn some money, but that wouldn't be enough to survive.

I tried not to panic. I tried to be reasonable and realize that I could still have a happy life. But the devastation of an empty life without love or dance consumed me. Suddenly, a sliver of hope emerged when I looked up and saw Will standing in front of my front door holding a huge bouquet of white roses.

"Why are you crying?" he asked.

"What are you doing here?"

"You first."

"Am I crying? I didn't realize..." I started rubbing the tears away from my face with the back of my hand as I sniffled. "How did you know where I lived?"

"I've always known. I never cared."

"Why are you here, Will?"

I wanted him to say that he knew it wasn't me and he was sorry that he hadn't spoken to me in a month and that he missed me and that he wanted me back but instead he said, "We need to talk. Can we go inside?" I shook my head. "I don't care what it looks like," he added softly. As I opened the door to let us in I prayed that the roaches would stay away and not embarrass me.

"Do you want to sit?" I said, offering the beat up couch hoping that he'd say no, but I don't even think he heard the question.

He placed the roses on the coffee table then ran his fingers through his hair. "I was so hurt when I saw that video," he started as if he was saying a rehearsed speech while he paced my tiny living room. "I couldn't get the sight of you giving yourself to David out of my head. Every time I

closed my eyes I saw it and it made me physically sick. I
didn't want you anymore. I didn't want to talk to you. I
didn't want to look at you. But I missed you. So, I tried to
put myself in your position. I tried to imagine what it would
be like to live in a place like this. I tried to understand how
your determination to get out could lead you to do something
like that, but I couldn't -"

"Will, please stop," I pleaded. I didn't want to hear
him go on about how much he hated me. It just made my
already miserable day even worse.

"No, I have to say this." His deep voice resonated
powerfully in the small space. "I couldn't understand how
you could do that, not you, not my angel. Then I realized
something. You wouldn't do that." My heart skipped a beat.
He knew it wasn't me. "So then I started to refuse to believe
what my eyes had clearly shown me," he continued still
pacing. His long stride covered the length of my living room
in almost one step. "I knew in my heart that you wouldn't do
that so I set out to prove it. I had to work on getting someone
to admit what they had done. I knew befriending David
wouldn't work. No one would believe that I'd ever talk to
that guy, so I decided to work on Ashley. I asked her out and
we started dating again. It took three weeks, a lot of coaxing,
and even more alcohol, but it worked. I got a full confession
on tape."

"What?" I said, leaping up from the couch. Will
thought he was helping, but he was making the situation
worse.

"I gave it to Headmaster Collins this morning. He
knows it was Sasha not you. He knows they set you up."

"Oh no, Will, no. Sasha will get expelled. She has to go to Princeton. She can't get expelled." I cried. Will grabbed me and held me in his strong arms. The arms that I missed and needed so desperately. I buried my face in his chest and just drank in his scent. I had dreamt about him holding me for a month and now his arms finally embraced me, but he was ruining everything. He was getting Sasha expelled.

"I'm glad you know it wasn't me, but we can't tell Headmaster Collins. I want to take the blame for her. She has taken care of me all these years and now it's my turn to repay her."

"You have to stop trying to protect her," he whispered into my hair.

"She's my sister. I'll do anything for her."

"There's something you need to know," he said as he pulled away from me and sat with me on that disgusting couch. "Sasha was in on it."

"What?" I leapt off of the couch.

"She set you up," he said gently easing me back down.

"She wouldn't do that to me."

"Yes, she would. She has everyone fooled into thinking she's this saint-like genius when she's really a vicious opportunistic manipulator. She is the brains behind David's cheating network. That's how she earns extra money."

"Will, don't say that," I pleaded. The Bitch Brigade had struck again. Ashley had obviously turned Will against my sister and she was trying to do the same to me.

"It's true. I know the whole story. Sasha is the Queen Bee. She's the leader of the Bitch Brigade. She has been using them and everyone around her to get what she wants. Remember Leila Baker the girl who had to transfer schools last year?" I nodded. "Sasha put the Bitch Brigade up to what they did to her. She was considering running against Sasha for student body president and she actually had a chance of beating her. And you know how Sasha is always studying and writing papers and stuff? Well, people go to David and tell him what assignment they need and Sasha does the work. She has written papers for probably half the population of Bridgeton."

"But why would she set me up? I never competed with her for anything."

"Listen," Will began to explain gently trying to take into consideration my feelings, "remember that note you found on your door?"

How could I forget? Those words were forever etched into my mind.

We don't know who you think you are. But anyone who lives in this hell hole isn't worthy of Bridgeton. Do what we say or you're gonna pay. - The Bitch Brigade

"Well, the note wasn't for you. It was for Sasha. They were sick of taking orders from her. But Sasha is not so easy to take down. She's got too much dirt on them. So, instead, they focused on you. She was legitimately pissed at them for attacking you. She had always made it clear that you were off limits. She wanted to expose them, but they rallied against her and threatened to reveal the cheating network that she had developed with David. Sasha couldn't let that happen. She knew she would get expelled and lose her chance at Princeton. The only way they agreed to not go after Sasha is if she helped them go after you. They made up that phony video and the phony Spanish test story. That's why they had to say it was a Spanish test. Spanish is the only class you have with seniors. Sasha knew that even if the evidence against you wasn't enough, that you would confess in order to save your beloved, precious sister."

I shook my head denying Will's words even though they really made sense.

"It's not possible. You have to call Headmaster Collins right now and tell him that you made a mistake." I tried to stand up, but Will pulled me back down to the couch.

"Look, how could David have thought it was you? If he really couldn't tell you two apart, how'd he know which one of you he gave the answers to? And then how would he know who to blackmail for that matter? And if he could tell you apart what was his motive for going after you and not everyone else he helped cheat? His story doesn't make any sense. He had to be in on it."

I kept shaking my head in protest. I didn't want to believe this about my sister.

"I know this is hard for you to believe, but it's the truth." Will knelt on the floor, held both my hands to his heart and with tears in his eyes said, "I wouldn't lie to you. I love you, Sony. You have no idea how much I love you."

"I love you, too," I said as I began sobbing uncontrollably. I didn't know whether I cried tears of joy because Will loved me again or tears of sadness because my sister was a fraud. But when he kissed me, it was clear as day what the tears represented. I didn't realize exactly how much I missed him until he placed his lips on mine. A wave of emotion overtook me.

"I missed you so much," he said, wiping the tears from my face. "I'm sorry I wasn't there for you all this time. I missed your audition, didn't I?" he asked as he took a look at my outfit for the first time. "How did you do?" he added. Mentioning the audition turned my tears of joy that I had Will back into tears of agony that I wasn't accepted into the DiRisio Academy.

"I didn't make it," I blubbered. "They saw the honor violation on my record."

Will held me in his strong arms. Then he kissed my forehead, my checks, my eyelids, every inch of my face as if he was a blind man trying to discover me with his lips. "We need to go see Headmaster Collins," he said after he had again focused on my mouth for a moment. "That's why I'm really here. He wants to talk to you. He tried calling but your phone is disconnected. I told him I'd come get you. Maybe he can help."

Chapter 28:
Picking Favorites

"Truth be told, I'm glad it wasn't you," Headmaster Collins said after telling me everything he had learned about Sasha.

"Sir?" I asked, only half listening to what he told me. I really didn't want to hear about all the awful things my sister had done.

"I said, I'm glad it wasn't you. Ever since the first time I met you I knew there was something different about you. I ask every potential student the same question: 'Why do you belong at Bridgeton?' You are the only one in 17 years to say that you didn't belong. You gave the most honest answer anyone has ever given to that question. That's why I wanted you to be a part of this school. I knew from that response that you had integrity." I had to think hard to remember what I had said on that day. I didn't realize that it had affected him so much.

"Your sister, Sasha, was an amazing student with

perhaps a flawless resume, but, to me, she had no substance, no soul. I've had my suspicions about her for some time. Of the two, you were always my favorite. I know I'm not supposed to pick favorites, but you are one of my favorite students in this entire school." For the first time Headmaster Collins seemed human to me. I couldn't believe that he liked me more than Sasha. It was comforting to hear. But my comfort level quickly diminished as he went back to his colonel tone, cracked his knuckles and said, "I know you come from a poor background and that you and Sasha had a difficult childhood. But is that basis enough to lie to me and the entire Bridgeton community?"

"I guess, at the time, I really didn't think of it as lying." I stared at my hands and played with my thumbs. "I just wanted to help my sister. She's the smart one, the one with the potential for a bright future. I thought her future was more important than mine."

Headmaster Collins sighed and said, "I hope one day you recognize what a remarkable individual you are. You have just as much potential as your sister. If anything, you have more because you're such a decent and unique person." He sighed again and shook his head. "I understand what you did for your sister. A part of me even admires you for it. It was brave. You sacrificed yourself for her. Unfortunately, lying, even for good reason, is still lying and I will not be able to accept you back into Bridgeton."

I nodded sheepishly still staring at my thumbs. Headmaster Collins' unwillingness to readmit me wasn't that much of a shock. I never even considered the possibility of returning to Bridgeton. My mind still ached over the death blow given to my dance career by not being accepted to

DiRisio.

"Mr. Maddox tells me you auditioned for The DiRisio Academy of Dance this morning." I nodded. "How did that go?"

I swallowed hard and said, "They complimented my talent, but disqualified me because of the honor violation." My voice was a hoarse whisper. I held back tears not wanting to cry in front of Headmaster Collins. I'd cried enough.

"Well that hardly seems fair. I think you've been through enough. Let me see what I can do." I looked up into Headmaster Collins' eyes. They had their normal intimidating intensity, but now, they also showed a sincerity that seemed almost…kind. For the first time that day, I felt a glimmer of security in my future. Somehow I knew Headmaster Collins could help with DiRisio.

"What did he say? What's gonna happen?" Will asked when I emerged from Headmaster Collins' office.

"He's gonna try to get me into DiRisio." I said as I sought the comfort of his embrace.

"That's awesome. Why aren't you more excited?"

"Nothing's final yet. He just said he'd see what he can do."

"Well, it's as good as done then. Can you imagine anyone saying 'no' to Headmaster Collins?" Will smiled, trying to lighten my mood. And he did somewhat. I'd forgotten what a beautiful smile he had and how his blue eyes danced with delight whenever he looked at me. "Let me take you to dinner. We can talk about Rome and make plans." I couldn't help but smile at Will's optimism.

"I love you," I said after kissing him. "I love that you care about me so much that you went through all this trouble to prove my innocence. I love how you have no doubt that I'll eventually make it into DiRisio. I love how you make me feel about myself. I love all you've done for me. But, Will, I need some time to sort through all this stuff in my head. I need to find my sister and talk to her. Maybe she has a good reason for what she did to me. Maybe -"

"You can't possibly be thinking about forgiving her, can you? There's no excuse for what she did." Will stepped back and held me at arm's length. He didn't understand the bond I had with Sasha.

"She's my sister."

Will closed his eyes and sighed. "Fine, go home, relax for a few hours, try to find Sasha. I'll bring dinner to you around 8:30, okay? Call me if you need anything." Will walked me to the bus stop and gave me a long sweet kiss good bye.

I didn't have to search too hard to find Sasha. When I opened the apartment door, she was sitting at the kitchen table. During the entire bus ride home, I tried to imagine what she would say to me or what I would do. Nothing I imagined prepared me for what she actually said.

Chapter 29:
Monster

"So, I suppose Will told you everything?" Sasha said in a tone that I wasn't familiar with. A tone that sounded like defeat.

"Yeah, but I need to hear it from you." I walked to the table and took a seat across from her. She didn't look at me.

"Fine, I'm a lying, cheating, backstabbing bitch. Is that enough for you?" Sasha took out a cigarette, lit it and took a long greedy drag. She was obviously a frequent smoker.

"No, it's not good enough. I think you owe me an explanation," I said, staring at the cigarette like it was some kind of alien crawling out of her mouth. "When did you start smoking?"

"About three years ago," she answered, taking another puff.

"Three years? Three years! You've smoked for three years and I had no clue."

"There's a lot you don't know about me," she said, taking another cigarette out of the pack. She wasn't even finished with the one in her mouth and she already yearned to start another. She tapped the unlit cigarette on the table.

"Like what?" I pleaded. "I thought we were best friends. I thought we told each other everything."

"We *were* best friends, until you found dance. Then it was like you barely had time for me anymore. You always had auditions and camps and tours. Hell, you left me for an entire summer. You left me in Venton Heights for eight weeks! That's when I picked up this nasty habit." Sasha took the half finished cigarette out of her mouth and snuffed it out on the table as if she was going to quit forever.

"So, you were jealous of me?"

"No, I wasn't jealous of you," she said mockingly. "Well, not at first, anyway. I was happy for you. It was like you had a guaranteed way out. You are so good. Do you know that? You're the best dancer I've ever seen. You have this amazing talent that can take you anywhere in the world. And what do I have?"

"What do you have? Are you serious? You have a 2250 on the SAT's, you have a 4.0 GPA, you have a 5 on four different AP exams, and a scholarship to Princeton!"

"I didn't always have all that," she said, losing her resolve and lighting another cigarette. "It took me six years to get accepted to Bridgeton. Six years. Then you come along and get in after one application. And when I got there, everyone had the same grades as me or better. I still wasn't good enough. I was always going to be the poor little black girl from Venton Heights. I didn't want that. I wanted more. So, I started to find ways to get better grades. I wanted higher SAT scores, I wanted to be the best student there was. Somehow, I hooked up with David and -"

"You started cheating." I finished the sentence for her. She nodded.

"David and I came up with fool proof methods to get around teachers, proctors, even plagiarism detection technology. We used everything from camera phones to calculators to iPods to good old fashioned cheat sheets sewn into the lining of my skirt or David's blazer. I think at first, we just wanted to see if it could be done; if we could get away with it. Then it became a challenge to try more and more different techniques. It was like we got some sort of high every time we got away with something. It was intoxicating. Once we had our system perfected, we started using it to make money."

"Oh, Sasha, how could you?"

"Oh, don't give me that," she snapped. "I did what I had to do. Everyone does it." Sasha started opening and closing her lighter. She'd stare at the flame then snuff it out with the lid. "I would do anything to get out of living in this place. I didn't mean to drag you down with me." She continued staring at the flame. She didn't look at me. She hadn't looked at me the entire time. I had hoped it was because she was sorry for what she'd done. I hoped that the desperation which caused her to behave so maliciously had turned into shame and remorse. I wanted her to cry and apologize and hug me and say that everything was going to be alright. But that didn't happen.

"I should've known something was up when Will got back together with Ashley," she said. "Even David warned me. I guess I underestimated his feelings for you." Sasha finished her cigarette and started another. "He really loves you. I wonder what that's like."

"What are you talking about? What about Desmond? He loves you."

"Desmond doesn't even know me, the real me. He was just a cover and I really couldn't care less about him."

"What?" My mouth flew open in a mixture of shock and disgust. Sasha's apparent double identity was more serious than I'd imagined. I felt sorry for Desmond. He couldn't have been more sweet and kind to her and she now talked about him like some sort of worthless fashion accessory.

"Sex with Desi is like having your teeth cleaned. It was an inconvenience but it had to be done to keep up the look I wanted. Unfortunately, I'm in love with David. But I couldn't go around telling people that because he's such an asshole. Sex with him was just as exciting as the cheating. Sometimes more. It was an exhilarating rush." I covered my ears like a child not wanting to hear the gory details of her illicit affair with the boy I once idolized, but she kept going. She saw how uncomfortable it made me, but she kept describing with horrifying explicitness her relationship with David. "Sometimes we'd mix the two and do it in the locker room during a test we happened to be cheating on. Once, I used Desi's car to go pick up a pizza. On the way, I stopped at David's house and we had sex in the backseat. David actually made me call Desi while we were doing it and had me ask him if he wanted pepperoni."

Sasha closed her eyes, let out a long puff of smoke and smiled as if she relived the encounters. "What he said about the video camera is true. He does keep a hidden one in his room. That's how I knew about Lauren DeHaven and Brooke and that David cheated on me with Colbert."

"Wait, Colbert?" I interrupted her remembering her supposed good friend who was now wasting away in some rehab clinic as part of her probation. "Did you have anything to do with her arrest?"

Sasha sighed and said, "I did what I had to do. She knew David was mine. She had no right." I shook my head. What kind of a person was she? I wished I could have turned around and run out of the apartment so as not to hear the awful things she told me, but pure shock had cemented my feet to the ground and forced me to sit there and learn the dreadful truth. "After a while, David and I got bored and had to try riskier things. David got a hold of some prescription drugs that we started selling and I found someone in Venton Heights that sold marijuana." She fell silent and reflective for a while and just smoked her cigarette.

"What about your hair?" I asked staring at her long beautiful locks that I now knew was a wig. "Did Lauren, Brittany, and Ashley really put Nair in your shampoo?"

Sasha rolled her eyes. "Don't be stupid, Sonya. Don't

you think I'd be able to smell Nair a mile away?"

"Don't call me stupid, Sasha."

She ignored me and said, "I fell asleep smoking a cigarette and set my hair on fire."

"And you're calling *me* stupid?" I folded my arms in a satisfied gloat.

Sasha glared at me. "Princeton is revoking my acceptance," she said as she stood up from the table. "But, you knew that would happen, didn't you? You had to know Bridgeton would expel me and I wouldn't be going to Princeton."

"Oh, wait, so now you're saying this is my fault?" I stood as well and returned her glare. "You're unbelievable! It's David's fault, then it's Will's fault, then it's the Bitch Brigade's fault and now it's mine? When are you gonna take responsibility for your own actions, Sasha?"

"Don't lecture me, Sonya. You have no idea the kinds of sacrifices I've made for you. I got you into Bridgeton, I kept your grades up, I protected you from the Bitch Brigade for as long as I could. I've taken care of you all your life and you couldn't do this one thing for me."

"Are you insane? You purposely set me up, humiliate me in front of the entire school, make my boyfriend think I'm a whore, and you have the nerve to be mad at *me*?"

"It was for the best!" Sasha slammed her fist against the table.

I couldn't believe she expected me to take the fall for her willful treachery. It was one thing when I thought she had just made a mistake, that she had fallen into a trap laid by David. But now, I saw her for what she really was.

"You mean it was the best for you," I said softly.

Sasha rolled her eyes and huffed, "Forget it." She reached down and picked up a suitcase that I hadn't even noticed.

"I'm gone," she said coldly heading toward the door.

"What?"

"I can't stay here. I'm done with Venton Heights, I'm done with Bridgeton, I'm leaving."

"But, where are you going?"

"Doesn't really matter as long as I get out of here," she shrugged. "I've got money and there are plenty of people who owe me favors. Don't worry about me. I'll survive." She locked eyes with me for a moment and I saw a sad little girl who didn't feel she was good enough. A little girl whose inner strength I used to envy, but now I despised.

Without saying another word, Sasha turned, walked out the door, and out of my life.

Chapter 30:
Payback's a Bitch, Bitch

Each year, the night before graduation, Bridgeton seniors got together at Fletcher Field for the senior campfire. The tradition started about nine years ago as one last opportunity for the seniors to bond before saying goodbye to each other perhaps forever. They sit around a fire, share stories of their years together, and watch the senior slide show projected on a huge screen like a drive-in movie.

"You sure you wanna do this," Will asked as we drove out to the field located 15 miles outside of town.

"Yeah, I'm positive." I looked down at Will's laptop and put the final touches on my little presentation.

"What about you, Emmaline? Are you ready for this?" I asked, looking into the back seat. Emmaline nodded and stared out the window. I could tell she was nervous about what we were going to do.

This year, the senior slide show wouldn't be filled with warm fuzzy memories of middle school class trips or elementary school plays. This year, the Bridgeton senior class was going to get an eyeful of what a few of their fellow classmates were really like.

The night of Sasha's confession, she not only left a void in my life where my sister and best friend used to be, she also left me a memory stick filled with everything David had ever captured on his hidden bedroom camera. That spliced with Ashley's taped confession made for one compelling slide show. Of course, I wouldn't show the explicit parts. The backstabbing, conniving conversations were enough.

In this video, Ashley, Brittany, Lauren, Sasha, Colbert, and David discussed plans on how to trap or attack nearly every student at Bridgeton. The Fat Tuesday prank was just the tip of the iceberg. They individually or collectively sabotaged people's grades, relationships, even college applications. They systematically made private information public or planted rumors and lies to gain control of whomever they wished. Sometimes their motives were clear, like in the case of Leila Baker; Sasha and Colbert wanted the presidency and vice-presidency. But, sometimes, they wreaked their havoc just for fun.

I didn't have any proof of what they did to Emmaline, but hopefully her personal testimony would be convincing enough.

When we arrived, the party was in full swing. There was no alcohol due to the security measures taken by Headmaster Collins, but from the hugging and laughing going on, I could tell everyone was still having a good time; that was until they saw me. A hush fell over the crowd as I walked towards the makeshift DJ area that housed the music and the LCD projector.

"Why is she here?"

"What does she think she's doing?"

"She's a junior."

"She's a cheater." I heard them whispering.

I felt their stares piercing my flesh trying to break down my resolve. But I continued until I had my video loaded. I found a microphone that I assumed was supposed to be used for karaoke later and said, "Bridgeton seniors, may I have your attention please." At this point, everyone who wasn't already staring at me now was, including Ashley, Brittany, and Lauren who had scrambled to the front of the crowd. "I know I'm not your favorite person right now. I know you think I've let you down. I just want to say, it's not what you think. I've been deceived as have many of you. My own sister blinded me, she blinded us. She has now been expelled as have Colbert Thornton and David Winthrop. But there are still three here among us that have not faced the music. If you think about the things that have been happening at this school and the three…*ladies* that always seem to come out on top, I think you'll figure out who they are. But just in case you're not sure, I've prepared a little presentation." Lauren dashed towards me, but Will held her back. Brittany clutched her stomach with one hand and covered her mouth with the other as if she wanted to puke. Ashley was too shocked to move.

The video played for an agonizing four minutes. They saw Ashley's drunken confession of the made up Spanish test scandal. They saw Lauren and Brittany laughing hysterically about breaking up Hayley and Michael over fake text messages from a made up girl. They saw Lauren and Sasha plotting to edit teacher recommendations from the college counseling office so Jennie, Lewis, Rachel, Grady and Clark wouldn't get accepted to Princeton and Sasha would be the only one this year. They saw Sasha actually hack into the school's grading system and change Susie's and Min's grades so they wouldn't get into any college. They saw Colbert and Ashley make a bet to see how many boyfriends they could steal.

Then Emmaline took the microphone and explained her ordeal with them. She told everyone how they attacked her because she got the lead part in the school play over Brittany. They used David to lure her into a stairwell under the ruse of going over lines, then they stripped her, and vandalized her car. The next day she transferred giving Brittany the lead in the play.

When it was over, no one said a word. I heard sniffling and saw tears from girls who had been personally affected by the antics. Guys who had been duped into cheating on their girlfriends or who were rejected from Princeton stood with their eyes wide and mouths agape. Slowly, every eye turned away from the screen and toward the Bitch Brigade.

"We're sorry, we didn't mean to hurt anyone," Brittany said.

"That's not what it looked like," someone yelled.

"It was Sasha, it was all Sasha," Lauren said.

"Yeah, she made us do it!" Ashley added. Someone threw a cup at the girls and more trash soon followed.

As Ashley, Brittany and Lauren retreated to their car amidst boos and derogatory names, I yelled into the microphone, "Payback's a bitch, bitch!"

Bridgeton cheered.

The next day, at Bridgeton's graduation, students hugged me and offered their apologies for ever doubting my innocence. They also told me horror stories of mysterious events that happened over the years that they now knew were instigated by the Bitch Brigade. I felt so loved and appreciated. It was the most comfortable I'd ever felt at Bridgeton. I could sit in the audience and enjoy my boyfriend's graduation without feeling out of place or targeted by Ashley, Brittany, and Lauren.

At this point, I was thinking things couldn't get any better. But they did.

Chapter 31:
'till Rome

"Thanks for coming today, babe." Will said as we walked through Venton Heights hand in hand. He looked completely out of place with his sun-bleached hair, crisp white shirt, and baggy khakis, but if he was the slightest bit uncomfortable, he didn't show it. He smiled as he took his mortar board off and playfully placed it on my head. Either he didn't notice the extreme poverty I lived in or he didn't care. I felt so foolish for ever hiding it from him.

"Of course I came. I wouldn't have missed your graduation." I kissed Will's hand. When we reached the front steps of my apartment building, Will stopped and planted a kiss on my lips so powerful it nearly lifted me off my feet. I didn't want it to end. Then I thought about something. It didn't have to end. "Do you want to come upstairs? No one's home," I breathed when he let me up for air. My body tingled with the thought that in a matter of moments, we could be physically showing our love for one another. Will's eyes widened as he nodded speechlessly.

Bubbling with excitement and anticipation, we raced each other up the stairs. Will kissed the back of my neck while unzipping my green summer dress as I fumbled with the lock. At last the door opened, but our dream of an afternoon of love making closed.

"Mom!" I yelped as soon as I stepped through the door. I discreetly zipped my dress up while Will greeted my mother.

"It's so nice to finally meet you, Mrs. Garrison," Will said, extending his hand and smiling nervously. My mother stared at his hand then raised her left eyebrow. Will's smile waned as my mother continued to disregard his hand. A nervous twitch developed in my stomach. What if she didn't like him? What if she treated him like Julia had treated me?

"After all I've heard about you, young man, you better put that hand away and give me a hug." My mother stood on her tip toes and wrapped her arms around Will's neck. I could see the relief wash over his face as he returned the embrace. "Thank you for everything you've done for my daughter."

"What are you doing home, Mom? Shouldn't you be at work?"

"Yeah, but shouldn't you be in a dance class?"

"I went to see Will graduate. I was going to try to catch a four o'clock pas de deux class or something."

My mother looked at her watch and said, "It's 3:15."

She looked at me, then at Will, then back to me. "I doubt if you would've been done in time."

"Mom!" I whined. Will turned completely red. How mortifying!

"Anyway," she said, smiling as she walked to the kitchen table. "The truth is, I wanted to talk to you." Her face turned serious as she sat down and gestured for me to join her.

"Do you want me to come back later or something?" Will started inching his way toward the door.

"No, you can hear this too." My mom bit her bottom lip as if deep in thought. I could tell she was searching for the right words. "Sonya, I want to apologize to you for not being a better mother."

"Mom, you don't have to apologize. You've had to work. I know -"

My mother held up her hand, cutting me off.

"Working is no excuse for not knowing my own daughters. I should've made time for you. Maybe I'm to blame for the way Sasha turned out."

"Mom, she fooled all of us."

Will crossed his arms as if to say Sasha never fooled him.

"In any case, I want to be a better mother. I want to get to know you. I want us to be close."

I got up from the table and wrapped my arms around her.

"So that means you're going to have to call me at least once a week while you're in Rome."

"Rome? Mom, didn't I tell you I got rejected from DiRisio?"

"Really? Then why would they send you this?" With a gleeful smirk she handed me a business sized envelope.

I think I might have passed out if Will hadn't stepped up behind me and placed his hands on my shoulders. He gently massaged the tension away as I stared in disbelief at the envelope that contained my future.

"Well, read it already!" My mother yelled after I held the envelope with trembling hands for thirty seconds without making the slightest attempt to open it.

"I can't."

"Well, if you won't, I will." She snatched the envelope from me.

"No, I can do it." I grabbed it back, took in a deep breath, and opened it.

We are pleased to inform you…

I screamed, Will screamed, my mother screamed. I started crying uncontrollable tears of relief and elation as Will gathered me in his arms.

"I'm going to Rome, I'm going to Rome," I chanted

on the verge of hyperventilating. I looked over at my mother who was crying as well. I handed the letter to Will as my mother and I hugged and danced around the apartment.

"Oh my God," he said suddenly.

"What?"

"You didn't read the rest of the letter."

"Why? What does it say?" I snatched the letter away from Will and anxiously read it over. What if I was wrong? What if they hadn't accepted me after all?

"It says that The DiRisio Dance Company has three weeks left in its US tour and they want you to be a temporary understudy before you start the academy. They...they want you to be in San Francisco...tomorrow." Will plopped himself into a chair at the kitchen table and ran his fingers through his hair.

"Tomorrow?" My mother and I said in unison. Sure enough I looked in the envelope and found a plane ticket with my name on it for June 8th. Tomorrow.

"I can't believe they expect me to be ready tomorrow."

"I can't believe I have to let you go for three weeks when I just got you back." Will grabbed my hand, pulled me into his lap, and held me tightly.

"Well, this is just ridiculous. You're gonna have to call those people and tell them you're not ready. They're gonna have to wait," my mother said with her hands on her hips.

"Mom, I can't do that. Do you know how lucky I am that they're taking me at all?"

My mother pursed her lips holding back another flood of tears. She blinked rapidly and with a shaky voice said, "Well, if you're leaving tomorrow, we have a lot to do tonight. I'm calling in to work. Will, do you by any chance have a cell phone I can use?" Will nodded and took his phone out of his pocket.

"I got an idea," Will said excitedly after my mother had left the room. He still held me in his lap. "Why don't I go with you? I'll get a plane ticket and my own hotel rooms and follow you around for the next three weeks."

"You and I both know that's not going to work. Don't you have to be in Rome on the 15th anyway?" He nodded sheepishly.

"It's just, I'm really gonna miss you."

"It's only three weeks and then we'll be together in Rome." I lifted his chin and kissed him on his adorably full pink lips. "You know what?" I said with a seductive grin. "Since tonight is our last night together for a while, why don't we make it special? You want to spend the night?" Will's eyes expanded.

"With your mom here? No way."

"Well, let's go to your place." I kissed his neck.

"Julia is probably home. Look, we'll just wait, okay?

We can consummate our love and our new life together at the same time. The first chance we get in Rome I'll make you a candlelit dinner, we'll dance under the moonlight, then make love by the fire over, and over, and over again." Will punctuated each thought with a kiss stirring a desire in me so great I wanted to rip his clothes off and take him right there in the chair.

"Well, if you expect me to wait until Rome, you better stop kissing me," I said playfully. I stood up, smoothed the wrinkles out of my dress and went to the refrigerator.

Will crept up behind me, closed the refrigerator door, and swept me up into his arms. He planted a kiss on my lips so strong, sensual, and tender I nearly went limp. Then, with a knowing gleam in his eyes, he whispered, "Till Rome."

And now for a sneak peek at book 2 of the Dancing Dream series.

The

Devil

of

DiRisio

The Devil of DiRisio

"Uh oh," my roommate Anna Marie said one Sunday morning. She had already gone for a jog, gotten breakfast, taken a shower, and now sat in bed reading one of her many tabloid magazines and newspapers. I still hadn't gotten out of bed. I was so exhausted all the time. I didn't know how Anna Marie had so much energy.

"What is it?" I asked with the pillow still over my head.

"Um, nothing, never mind," she said.

I rolled over too tired to try and force a piece of gossip out of her. It was probably another rumor about who Damian Karl, the new choreographer, was sleeping with now. "It's just that, where did you say Will was last night?" Now she had piqued my interest. What did she know about my Will?

I removed the pillow and sat up. "He had a game in Paris."

"Well, according to this picture, he was in Florence getting into a limo with Veronica Valerio." I flung the covers off, hopped out of bed, and snatched the newspaper out of her hand. I couldn't believe my eyes, but I had to. That was definitely Will and that was definitely Veronica Valerio, a.k.a the singing slut. Who in the world gave that tone deaf Barbie doll a record contract anyway? But they were just getting into a limo. It didn't mean anything. Well, it did mean that Will had lied to me. Again.

"What does it say?" Anna Marie asked since she still couldn't read Italian. I skimmed the article. It basically claimed that they were an item now. Neither of them had confirmed the relationship, but they had been seen together on several occasions including at her Tuscan Villa.

"Nothing," I lied. "Can I borrow this?"

"Sure, I have more." Anna Marie settled in on her bed and opened a Teen People magazine with none other than Veronica Valerio on the cover. I wanted to tear it to shreds, but I held back. Maybe there was a perfectly logical explanation for all this.

I used my key and entered Will's house as quietly as possible. I went into his bedroom and found him still sleeping at 1:00 in the afternoon. That wasn't like him. Usually, he got up at the crack of dawn to jog or lift weights. He was obviously exhausted from his long night of partying with Veronica Valerio. I couldn't believe he was cheating on me. I got so angry I jumped on the bed and started beating him with the rolled up newspaper like he was a misbehaving dog. He woke up confused and instinctively swatted me away. I fell to the floor but jumped right back up and continued my assault.

"What are you doing?" he asked as he held me back with one arm.

"Did you think I wouldn't find out or did you think I was just stupid?"

"What are you talking about?"

"Don't play dumb, Will." I stopped swinging at him long enough to show him the picture in the paper.

"Oh," he said. I lunged at him again. He caught me and slammed me down on the bed. He had my arms pinned at my stomach so I kicked at him. He used his knee to pin down my legs. He was so big. When did he get so big?
"It's not what you think."

"Oh, it's not? Then what is it Will? You lied to me. How could you? I love you." I broke down and started crying pathetically. Will sat me up and held me as I let the tears flow onto his bare chest. "You said you were in Paris. How did you end up in Florence with Veronica?"

"I *was* in Paris. The game was in the afternoon. We won, so some of the guys wanted to celebrate. One of my teammates owns a club in Florence so we went. Veronica was there. After a few hours, she offered to fly us back to Rome on her private jet. I wasn't the only one in that limo. Nothing happened."

"You swear nothing happened?" I sniffled.

"Baby, I swear on my parents' grave. Nothing happened."

I said I believed him even though I didn't.

***

"I'm actually glad you came over," he said as I sat on his kitchen counter while he made French toast. "I've been wanting to talk to you about something. Our schedules are so busy; we don't get to talk face to face a lot anymore. I'm worried about you. About your health," he said as he took our plates to the dining room. He sat down and started eating without finishing his thought. Why was he concerned about my health? My health was great. I was a dancer. I had to be healthy. Halfway through his breakfast he pointed to my untouched plate and said, "Are you gonna eat that?"

"You can have it. I already ate." I dumped my French toast onto his plate.

"You see, this is what I'm talking about."

"What?"

Will wiped his mouth with a napkin and said, "For a long time, all you did was eat, sleep, and dance. And I understand that. Dancing is your life. But lately, it seems like there's a lot more sleeping and dancing and a lot less eating."

"What are you talking about?"

"I haven't seen you physically bring food to your mouth in a month."

"Well, we're both busy. You said so yourself. We don't get to see each other that much. I eat when you're not around."

"I'd like to believe that, I would. But I've talked to Anna Marie. She hasn't seen you eating either."

"Well...I'm not with her all the time. I like to eat by myself."

"She says all you do is sleep."

"I'm tired. I dance twelve hours a day. Don't I have the right to be tired?"

"You've lost like 15 pounds. You're not healthy. You need help."

"Will, thank you for caring, but I'm fine. I am healthy. Madame Mara says I look better than ever."

"Just let me take you to a doctor. I'll do anything if you just see the team nutritionist."

I stared at him in disbelief. How could he think I was anorexic? I ate plenty. He was just trying to get my mind off the fact that he cheated on me with Veronica Valerio. I would've brought that up, but I didn't feel like fighting. I was too tired. So, instead, I took a piece of Will's French toast, slathered it with syrup and stuffed it in my mouth defiantly. The super sweet taste and thick texture made me gag. I wanted to puke, but I held it down. When Will went to get dressed, however, I couldn't hold it in any longer. It all came back up into his sink.

***

I felt lost and alone. I was convinced my boyfriend was cheating on me and he was convinced I was anorexic. All of my instructors thought I was a fat unskilled dancer. Even my roommate, my supposed best friend, had betrayed me. How could she tell Will I hadn't been eating? What did she know? I went back to my room and slept the afternoon away in a fitful sleep with frequent dreams of my life in Venton Heights. Was I any better off now than then?

I awakened to someone pounding on my door. I looked over at the clock. It read 8:45 although it felt like the middle of the night.

"I'm coming," I called as I crawled out of bed. The pounding continued. "Hold up, I'm coming." I opened the door and got the surprise of my life.

"Hey, little sis, I've missed you."

Proof

Made in the USA
Charleston, SC
23 March 2011